Sweetwater Tales

Aaron W. Kemp, M.D.

Aaron Kemp
04 02 04

VANTAGE PRESS
New York

This is a work of fiction. Any similarity between the names characters, and places in his book and any persons, living or dead, is purely coincidental.

Ccver design by Polly McQuillen

FIRST EDITION

Published by Vantage Press, Inc.
419 Park Ave. South, New York, NY 10016

Manufactured in the United States of America
ISBN: 0-533-14674-7

Library of Congress Catalog Card No.: 2003094532

0 9 8 7 6 5 4 3 2 1

Sweetwater Tales

Part I

Law Comes to Sweetwater

1

I remember when I saw him riding into town. He came from across the sagebrush by the south trail. I could tell from a distance he was a big man, riding a big black horse. He was trailing a small mule with a full pack. He rode right up to me like he knew where he was going, but I noticed he was looking around cautiously, slowly moving his head and eyes as if on guard against an unseen foe. *A cautious man*, I thought.

I ran the stable and blacksmith shop in Sweetwater. That had to be the worst name in the world for a town, because the water was horrible. Must have been someone's idea of a joke.

The day was hot and still, with a band of white puffy clouds looking like they were thrown against the sky—stuck and not moving. The dust was a foot thick in most places and as he approached, his animals raised a cloud of their own dust with their hooves.

He rode right up to me standing by my anvil under one of the only trees in town, a scrubby cottonwood at that, on its last legs to boot.

"Howdy-do!" I said. " Get off that horse and have a drink of cold water. I can't tell you from a tumbleweed with eyes. You got more dust on you than the top of my barn."

"Thanks, but I reckon I better water my animals first. They got me here. This old hoss carried me a long way and never complained a bit. Had to drag the damn mule, but he made it."

I pointed to the watering trough. He swung easily from the saddle, began brushing off the trail dust with his floppy hat, smiling like he had some secret. I noticed that he never stopped looking all around, taking in everything. He watered the horse and mule. They drew in great gulps through their partially open lips, pausing now and then to get a breath of air as the water dripped off their noses. When they had their fill, he led them over to the hitching rack and tied them loosely. He loosened the saddle girth on his big black gelding and also on the mule's packsaddle. They both hung their heads down some, lifted up a rear foot a little and hunched over in the resting position that horses always do, with their eyes three-quarters shut.

"Now, where's my water?" he asked as he sauntered over. I had a pretty deep well so the water wasn't bad. Best in town, anyway. I gave him the drinking dipper and pumped the water up for him. He took off his hat and poured the first two dippers right over his head and the third one right into his face. Then he gulped down two dippers of water before looking up.

"Man, I was dry inside and out."

I had a chance to sort of look him over, size him up. He was a big man all right, six feet. His face looked like it had been chiseled out of red rock, wind blown with cracked lips and all. Black streaked with gray stubble of a beard grew partly down his neck. He had a full head of hair, the same color as his beard, curling down the back of his neck. His eyes were deep blue and the most remarkable feature on him. The lines of expression created a constant quizzical smile.

"I want to board up my animals. You in that business?"

"Yup, sure am. Two bits a day for both. You staying long?"

"That's fine." He handed me fifty cents. "How long I stay depends. Do you know where the mayor might be?" he asked. He looked at a scrap of paper from his shirt pocket. "Someone named M. Fitz?"

"That's me, pardner, Marion Fitz, and I am the mayor, blacksmith, and owner of the livery stable and partners in the general store. You must be the Martin fellow coming to be town constable or marshall, right?"

"Well, I am George Martin all right and I did come here to inquire." He got a big silly grin on his face.

"Your name—Marion?"

I jumped back with mock hostility and clenched my fist in the air, "Something funny about my name? Want to make something of it?"

He looked at me and laughed out loud. It was a good laugh and I knew I would like this man.

"My god, no! Marion is a perfectly fine name. I wouldn't want to mix it up with you. I can tell you're way too tough for me to handle." He stuck out his big paw and we shook, chuckling to each other.

"My name is Marion all right but people call me Buck. When I was younger, I broke most of the wild horses people brought in, when my father ran this place."

"Well my name is George and people call me George. Though I have been called a lot of things."

"Well, Buck—Mayor Marion; what—Mayor Fitz, Mayor Buck?"

"Call me Buck."

"Buck then, can we put the animals up then get me a place to stay, a haircut, a bath, and something to eat—and then we will talk about the job?"

I agreed, stopped what I was doing at the forge and went over to the mule while George attended to his horse. He took the packsaddle off after removing the panniers on each side. The britchens were dry and tightly buckled but I managed to slip them off all right. The packsaddle was a good one, store bought, with the wood paddlers carved with leather on top and sheepskin underneath. I reached over and untied the lead rope from the hitching rack and started walking to the barn.

"Watch that son-of-a-bitch," George called out. "He bites."

Too late! The damn animal chomped on my shoulder and gave it a shake for good measure.

"OK—you no good ring-tailed shit-head."

George laughed quietly, not looking at me.

"Warned ya."

"Kind of late, don't ya think?

"If you cut this worthless piece of shit's balls off he would stop biting," I said rubbing the top of my bruised shoulder. "I'll be glad to do it for you."

"Nope," says George. "He keeps his balls. Gives him personality and makes him the best guard you ever saw around your camp at night. Always alert."

"Damn," I said. "Never heard of anything like that."

We put the horse and mule each in a stall with a big pile of meadow grass hay and a bucket of oats. Then headed toward town. First I grabbed the tin star I had made on the forge and put it in my shirt.

After we got into town, he went over to the barbershop, got himself a bath, a haircut and a shave. He pulled on the new clothes he bought at the store, shined his boots and we meandered over to the Coach House Cafe. By then it was 4:00 P.M. and the evening breeze began to cool things off a little—damn little. Our feet plopped in the dust as we went over to the Cafe without talking.

When we sat down, I noticed that he moved around so that his back was to the wall and then tucked his holster with the big .44 over his hip in front. He did these things without thinking about it, automatically, but deliberately. He was a man who took precautions and was used to watching his ass against unexpected threats.

Frances was a big, happy, round-faced half-Mexican

woman in her fifties. She seemed to always be wearing a smile. But, she was a tough and strong heifer who threw many rowdy cowboys right out the door, then collected her bill on the street whether they finished eating or not.

"Howdy, Frances. This here is George Martin, up from Texas. He's looking to be city constable, sheriff or marshall. Whatever he's called, the law for the people here anyhow."

"Hola, Meester Martin. You want to live awhile longer? No?"

"Hola, yourself, Frances. I aim to keep myself alive. Right now I am as hungry as a spring bear."

Frances' smile grew wider even as she poured us real coffee and brought silverware. She paused a second and brought two large red napkins. We sat drinking our coffee, not saying much at first. I looked at his hands, large with long fingers and smooth joints. Smooth palms, no calluses. This guy was no cowboy or trapper.

"Are you fast with that pistol?" I asked.

Before the word pistol was through, he held the barrel in my face. I never saw his hand fly. My god he was fast. My jaw dropped open and I started to say something. He smiled widely, twirled the gun two times around and dropped it in his holster.

"My finger wasn't on the trigger," he said.

"I'm glad! Can you hit anything?"

He made a big clumsy show of reaching for his pistol.

"I'll show ya."

"No, no. Show me later."

"Can you shoot, Marion?" he asked.

"Not with a pistol. I couldn't hit my own ass. I can drive nails with my rifle though."

Frances brought two large platters with broiled rib steaks with beans and fried potatoes piled on them.

"Hey Marion, let's eat!"

"Call me Buck," I said.

We dug in, George eating all of his then finished off half of my rib steak for me.

"That was good," said Big George, wiping his mouth with his napkin. "What's for dessert?"

Frances said, "Wait till you see this!" She returned with two slabs of apple pie still warm from the oven.

"I'm going to like this place," said Big George, not waiting to put his fork to work.

Clean-shaven with a new haircut, George looked a lot different all right, but his clear blue eyes were the same. He looked about thirty-five or so, but it was hard to tell because of his weather-worn face. He leaned back in his chair and became serious.

"Tell me the problem here; the truth and all of it. Don't leave off the bad parts, ya hear?"

I leaned back to answer, "This town is growing fast—too fast. The railroad put a spur into here about two years ago to take cattle east. You probably saw the trail herds on the outskirts of town, down in the valley there with the box canyon. Easy to keep the herds in there, lots of grass and the creek running through. The cowboys come in after the trail drives and tear the place up. Folks are afraid to go out when they are in town. They shoot the signs down, shoot the bar up, take over the saloon and raise hell with the girls at Lou's. We have a church here with a bell in a little tower. It has become a big sport to shoot the rope so the bell will fall. Hasn't happened lately, but that bell has a lot of dents, I'll tell you. We need to establish law and order."

George looked out the window at the town with a toothpick in the corner of his mouth. He looked directly at me, then with a wrinkled brow . . .

"What ain't you telling me, Marion, Buck? I want it all."

"You don't miss much, do you?"

"Hell, Marion, every cow town gets cowboy problems. They can be bad sometimes all right. Something else is going on here. What is it?"

I paused a minute, gathered my thoughts and replied as honestly and directly as I could.

"About two years ago, these Stouffer brothers rode in here, three of them. It didn't take long for everyone to be skeered of them. One of them, Hoss, is a big ugly man with a big ugly temper. He pushes everyone around for no reason. He beat the livin' hell out of the barber that used to be here because he nicked him a little shaving his punkin face. He is mean. He is not mentally all there and he is as big as you. His older brother, Rodney, is a fuckin' weasel who steals what he wants from the store and dares you to say anything. He is fast with a gun and fast with his mouth. He is a mean drunk. One time he cut up one of Lou's girls. She said it was because he couldn't get it up. Blamed her for it. He has killed two men in gunfights right in town for nothing other than bad words. He's a nasty bad man. The honcho of the three is that smooth-faced snake that runs the Silver Pit Saloon. He is a tinhorn gambler that cheats the poor, dumb cowboys when they are drunked up on his rotgut whiskey. The previous owner was Brad Pullen, also a sidewinder. He ended up dead in the alley with a small caliber gunshot wound between the eyes and Dude shows up with a marker for the saloon that is signed by Pullen the day before. Stunk to high heaven and hell and back. Anyone could have signed those papers."

I stopped talking and finished my coffee while Big George kept looking out the window. "Nothing else, Mayor Marion?"

"Damn it, call me Buck! Nothing else I can think of right off anyhow. Believe me, that's enough."

2

As mayor of Sweetwater (kind of a joke), I called a town meeting at the church that night and everyone in the whole darn town came. I just presented Martin to them and said if there were no objections, I was swearing him in as town constable and as soon as the governor approves, he will be territory marshall.

"Any questions?"

My partner, Pat Finn, stood up.

"What is your background and experience, Mr. Martin? I mean no disrespect." He smiled his half-tooth smile.

"No disrespect taken, Mr. Finn. Started out a private detective for Pinkerton out of Washington, D.C. Lots of bad things came down as a result of the war. Railroad land, ranch-and-range war mostly. I did not like what Pinkerton stood for, particularly in the mines and factories back east. I could not stomach it. Besides, I had a taste of the west and figured that's where I belong. I went to Texas where I served with the Texas Rangers. I have a letter of recommendation from Captain Stark and one from Houston himself. Now, any more questions? I am pleased to answer."

The mention of the Texas Rangers was enough. The approval was obvious. George continued on very good naturedly, smiling and being funny.

"I don't drink. Much anyway. I don't gamble at all because I always lose. Never saw an honest deck. I like a good cigar when I can get one, otherwise I roll my own. I keep in shape walking five miles a day, uphill if I can, but I can't quite find no hills close by here. I play the guitar a little, but I can't sing for sour apples."

People were laughing out loud. He was an easy guy to like.

"You mated, constable?" someone asked.

"Not at present," was his answer.

He let it go at that. I walked on over and swore him in as town constable with complete authority to enforce the law as he saw fit. That meant a lot of trust in his power. It was all written out beforehand, legal-like, by a young attorney in town named Fletcher. Then we both signed it and let anyone from town who wanted to sign also. Then I handed him the star I made and the place came apart laughing.

"My god, Marion. This thing is six inches across. If I wear it on the front of my shirt, it will pull me over frontward; and if I wear it on my back it will look like a target. I think I will pin it to the seat of my pants."

I looked over the laughing crowd and in the back I saw the Stouffer brothers: Rodney, Dude and Hoss. They glared back at me, mean as shit and not laughing.

Trouble is coming, I thought, *and soon!*

"George," I said. "Let's take a look at the jail that the last yahoo built here three years ago. Not that you are a yahoo, understand." I poked him with my finger in the belly. It was like hitting wood. He just looked at me and followed me down the street to the jail. It had actually been well made and designed. There was an office and a desk out front with the back split in half; jail on one side and living quarters on the other side with a stove, sink, hand-pumped water, nice bunks, over-stuffed chair, and a big horsehair sofa. There were even a couple of watercolor paintings on the wall that were awfully good.

"Who painted these?" George asked.

"The last lawman."

"What happened to him?"

"He and the doctor here in town got to be real good friends. They drank themselves silly every damn night. Then both of them fell madly in love with a woman. You already know Frances. She liked to screw with both of them. Not at once, I mean. She couldn't choose so they got all tanked up, all teary eyed and decided to fight it out. Can you believe it? They actually killed each other in the street. Frances cried for a month and wouldn't come out of her house. She quit drinking and stopped being a dance hall whore and opened the café. What a story, huh? They say she inherited a lot of coin from the doctor and she has it hid somewhere."

"Say, George, you know what? This is pretty small quarters here. I got a lot of room at my place. My wife died a few years ago and my boys are all growed and gone. Got a lot of room."

"Marion, that sure as hell is big of you, but I'll be fine by myself here, for a while at least. I am used to being by myself and anyhow I don't spend much time at home, but thanks. It's nice to know I have something to fall back on if I get cabin fever."

3

A couple of days later, a trail drive ended up outside of town. The cowboys were all west Texas wildcats. A dozen of them came into town just at dark. Things were reasonably quiet for a long time but by midnight the ones that weren't out cold were raising all kinds of hell. Four guys went over to Frances' Café and beat on the door for service. When she refused, they pushed their way in, broke up a bunch of furniture and dishes and shot up the ceiling. They were about to light the place on fire when Frances got to her double-barrel shotgun and ran them out. Big George heard the gunshots into the ceiling and came running in time to see the cowboys riding off back to their camp.

"You all right, Frances?"

"Yeh, but look at my place. Who's going to pay for this?" Big George looked around with a deep frown.

"Those assholes," he said under his breath. "They are going to pay for it. Must be fifty dollars worth of damage. I'll pay them a visit in the morning. They will pay for it all right."

4

The next morning at sunup, George was just cinching his saddle up when I rode up to the barn. I had my 30-30 in my saddle scabbard and a 25-30 across my lap. Both Winchester model 64 carbines loaded all the way.

"Howdy, Sheriff," I said without dismounting.

He looked at me quizzically and said, "Howdy yourself." He finished cinching up, then swung himself aboard his big gelding. The horse was well trained and didn't move until he wanted to.

Finally he looked at me, up and down, noting the rifles.

"Where are you going, hunting with two rifles?"

"Nope. Not going hunting. I'm going with you. I appointed myself deputy constable." He didn't say anything, just sat on his horse and looked at me with the plainest face I ever saw.

"Could be dangerous."

"I'm bored."

"You could get a hole bored into you."

"Frances is my friend. So are you."

"Well, hell. Let's go then but you do what I tell you—understand?"

"OK," I said and fell in behind him.

The cow camp was about five miles out of town with the cattle herded up in the blind canyon, a large one, with lots of grass and water.

George's big horse was a tremendously athletic and energetic animal. His long legs and long pasterns made for easy riding. My poor damn mustang had to keep a constant trot to keep up with his fast walk.

It was a beautiful fall morning with no breeze at all to disturb the colored leaves up in the occasional cottonwood groves. Here and there a jackrabbit would fly out of cover and hightail it across the sage. The trail was wide and the land was flat. We made good time and soon were on a rise looking down into the camp.

The boys were gathered around the chuck wagon squatting on the ground eating their morning meal. Mushy Johnny cakes, bacon and dried apples, washed down with bitter black coffee. Their life was hard. Long hours in the saddle pushing a herd of stupid stubborn cattle through all kinds of weather and terrain. No wonder at the end of the drive they tended to over celebrate and get wild. They were good guys, really, but all wound up. I wondered if George knew this.

We stopped and observed the layout.

"Marion, I see the ramrod of the outfit standing by the fire there, giving orders. You take that peashooter you call a rifle (He meant my 25-35 carbine) and go over to the chuck wagon. Get some coffee, make small talk, and cover my back. Some of those guys are carrying pistols."

I nodded and did as I was told. I felt like I was riding into a beehive.

George yelled hello as we started down the small hill. The cowboys looked up at us coming and none of them smiled or waved. I rode over to the chuck wagon. Got off my pony with the rifle in my hand, said howdy to the cook and nodded friendly-like to the cowboys. Some nodded back or made little waves with their free hands, but most just kept on eating. There were about a dozen. Most of them were young men—but there were two older guys and two black cowboys nearby.

Big George rode up to the ramrod of the outfit and for the first time I saw the big star fastened to his shirt, exposed by his now-open trail coat.

"Howdy, Sheriff," the ramrod said, taking a step or two toward him. "That's a hell of a badge you got there," not smiling.

"Howdy-do. Where you boys coming from?" George asked.

"North Texas. Name's Goodnight. What the hell have my boys done to deserve this visit, or are you just being friendly so early in the morning?

"Both, Goodnight. I am a friendly man and Sweetwater is a friendly town. But we've got a problem," George said. Then let the silence fall.

"Get down off your pony. Sam, bring the sheriff a cup of coffee." A young cowboy by the fire grabbed a tin cup from the chuck wagon, filled it with steaming coffee, and handed it to George as he slid from the saddle.

"Obliged," said George.

The cowboy just nodded and walked back to the fire.

"What's the problem, Sheriff—uh, I didn't catch your name?"

"I didn't throw it. Name's George Martin and that's my deputy Buck Fitz over there."

I waved and smiled but no one even looked at me.

"These are good boys, Martin, just maybe a little rank now. What did they do?"

"Why hell, I know they are. I made the trail ride from Texas to Montana when I was sixteen. When I wasn't freezing, burned by the sun, filled with dust, bone-weary tired and full of self-pity, I was full of piss and vinegar. When we got to a town, it was like life starting again. I know."

Goodnight grinned from ear to ear and reached out to shake hands. I could feel a change in the atmosphere. The cowboys began talking and joking with each other and moving about.

"Seems some of your boys got hungry last night about midnight and tried to rustle some grub at the café. They was a bit hard on the place. Broke some dishes and chairs and shot a few holes in the ceiling. Didn't get anything to eat either."

"Damn it!" said Goodnight. "You guys hear what he says?" He was red-faced and angry. "Red, I know it was your ornery doins. Who the hell went with you?"

A wiry cowboy with red hair and freckles stood up with his hat in his hands and a half-smile on his face. He looked comical, and everyone including me and George had a little chuckle.

"I don't remember, Cap. I was howlin' at the moon."

Meaning he was drunk. With this everyone except Goodnight laughed out loud. He looked like a good-natured guy really—all freckle-faced and sunburnt.

"We will settle this thing," says Goodnight. "How much damage was done anyhow?"

"Fifty bucks will cover it." George said quickly.

"Fifty bucks! What in hell?" Goodnight went from foot to foot in his anger, kicking up dust. He turned to his boys and shook a fist in the air.

"Got an idea for you, Captain," says George.

"What?"

"All those boys," nodding toward the cowboys, "is partially to blame for egging them on and getting unruly with them. That right, ain't it boys?"

The cowpokes pushed their hands in their pockets and moved around mumbling to each other.

"Pay me forty bucks then deduct two dollars off at the payoff. From everyone mean. Then the innocent ones can get squared away with the wild bunch on their own."

Goodnight looked like he approved and ambled slowly

over to the wagon. “You said it was fifty dollars.”

“We will settle for forty dollars, cash money, now.”

Goodnight dug around in the chuck wagon and came out with two twenty dollar gold pieces, walked over and gave them very quickly to George.

“Thanks,” says George. “The matter is closed.”

“You are a fair man, Sheriff.”

“So are you, Goodnight. When you come to town, I would want to buy you a drink.” He mounted up. His horse spun around for him and he started off, then stopped, looked over his shoulder. “Worse damn coffee I every drunk,” he said. “Besides, can’t drink hot coffee from a tin cup. But thanks anyhow. One other thing, when the boys come into town, leave their shootin’ irons here in camp. No guns allowed in the city limits,” he said matter of fact. I was beside him then and we just walked our horses right out of there without looking back.

He rode on in silence for about a mile, then I says, “That gun rule—that applies to everybody?”

“Everybody but you and me, Deputy.”

I saw trouble coming again. He would have to get the guns away from three bad hombres I know of. That wasn’t going to go smooth.

5

After we got back to town, we put our horses up, had breakfast over at the cafe with Frances at the cookhouse. When we moseyed over to the newspaper, Calvin was already there setting type for the weekly newspaper. He was a friendly little red-faced, puffy German who had a smile always like it was painted on his face. I liked him. So did everyone.

"Howdy, Calvin. You know the constable, George?" I says.

"Ya. I think so."

He shook hands with George quickly without making much eye contact and developed a quizzical look on his face. "What can I do for you?" he asked.

"I just need some posters printed up. Can you do it?"

"What you say?" asked Calvin.

"Here is what I want." George reached into his pocket and brought out a piece of paper and presented it over to him. Calvin read it, then looked up at George and the smile reappeared on his pink face.

"How many? Two dozen?"

George just nodded.

"I take time now. You have them in two hours. You don't pay anything either. My duty."

"Thank you, sir. That is right good of you." George said with a grin. By that afternoon, we had signs all over Sweetwater.

STARTING SUNDOWN
NO GUNS ALLOWED IN SWEETWATER

GUNS WILL BE CONFISCATED
$50.00 FINE TO GET THEM RETURNED
IN 24 HOURS
BY ORDER OF GEORGE MARTIN, CONSTABLE
NO EXCEPTIONS
CHECK ARMS AT THE JAIL OFFICE
ALSO—NO HIDDEN KNIVES OR CLUBS

The next day was Saturday and a few cowboys came into town. The boys who could not read had the sign read to them. All of them trudged on over to the jail and left their pistols there with no complaints at all. It went well. We gave them a receipt and tagged their weapons with their names.

One young tough started to grumble some but surrendered his pistol with a reluctant grin. "If no one else has got one, I guess I don't need one neither."

"Have a good time, cowboy," said George. "No fightin' either. You look tough as stirrup leather." The scrawny kid liked that and left good-naturedly. I said it went well. It did until after siesta time—about 3 P.M.

George was watching out the window, sort of waiting. I looked out and there the three of them were—the Stouffer brothers, Dude, Hoss and Rodney—walking right down the middle of the street with wise-ass looks on their faces.

"Bring your rifle. The big one. Looks like we got work to do," George said as he put his glasses on. I grabbed my rifle and got to my feet and started to the door with George.

"Cock it," he said glancing back at me. "Keep it ready. Cover Rodney and watch my back."

We clomped out on the porch just as they got even with the jail, them being in the middle of the street.

"Come to check in your guns? Good. We don't want no trouble."

Hoss and Rodney stopped where they were and turned

toward us. The Dude just walked away slowly to the other side of the street. No one said anything at all for a couple of minutes. I had my rifle held loose with the barrel pointing down at Rodney's feet with my finger wrapped around the trigger. Hoss stepped forward a little and Rodney took a step or two back. My rifle followed him and he knew it. It was cocked and he knew that too.

"Well now, sheriff, you think I'm gonna check my guns?" His smile was like a snake.

"You're gonna check them or I'm gonna take them and you will pay fifty dollars or you ain't getting them back. You should have just left them at home."

"You're gonna take them? You're gonna take them? How you think you're gonna do that?"

"I'll blow your fuckin' head off if I have to! I'm the law now."

"No four-eyed son-of-a-bitch is going to take my guns—law or no," he said with a sneer.

He started to make a move toward his gun—just started, mind you—when George's gun cleared leather, spoke out and damned if Hoss's hat didn't fly off his head like it had wings. Rodney sort of jerked, but he saw my rifle pointed right at his heart and never reached. Hoss just stood there with his mouth opened and staring. He looked scared. He looked scared! He was scared!

"Drop your gun belt, pig face," George ordered. Hoss hesitated.

"Now, you fat pig!" said George. He was mad as hell.

Hoss undid his buckle and let the gun belt drop to the ground. George walked over, facing him, as he put his own gun up in his holster.

"You called me bad names. Four-eyed what? You don't like my glasses. I'll take 'em off." He slowly and deliberately took them off and put them in his shirt pocket. "We need to understand things around here," said George.

"You son-of-a-bitch," said Hoss, almost under his breath. He shouldn't have said that. George's left struck out with hell fury and caught Hoss right in the belly under his breastbone. The air went out of him with a whoosh. He doubled right over as George's right fist pounded with a thud, an uppercut strong as a mule's kick. Hoss' nose split, smashed all over his ugly face. He staggered back with his hands on his face but didn't fall until a left cross tore into his cheek and eye. He laid out there, tossing around moaning, bleeding and doubled. George looked over at Rodney. He slowly reached down and unbuckled his gun belt without saying anything. Big George walked over to the Dude standing on the sidewalk on the other side of the street. They glared at each other.

"I want the little pistol you carry in your coat. The Derringer." George held out his hand. Dude just glared at him without moving, not saying nothing. George just slowly doubled up his fist hard as a rock. Dude looked at it, then opened his coat. Quick as that, George snatched the Derringer himself.

"Give me the knife in your boot."

"What knife?" Dude acted surprised.

George drew his pistol so fast you could hardly see it and poked it in his face. Dude pulled back his head but didn't move to his boot.

"Now or I will blow your foot clean off," George said between his teeth, as he let a shot go right between Dude's feet, blowing splinters all over. For the first time, Dude looked scared. He was shaking all over like a shitting dog. As he reached down, pulled up his pants leg and took the knife out of its boot sheath, George took it from him, stared at him a second, then gave him an open-handed slap on the face like he was paddling a kid's ass. God, his face turned red and for a minute or two you could see the finger marks.

"Now, you Stouffers get the hell off the street and out of here before you make me mad."

6

It's funny sometimes the way things come down. My partner in the mercantile store comes up to me out of the blue and tells me he can't stand being a storekeeper anymore and he is leaving to go prospecting in the Superstition Mountains.

"You can have it all. I don't want no part except grubstake supplies. Then, I'm gone."

Well, Bill had the gold fever right bad. I could see burning in his eyes. I knew there was no talking him out of it. I didn't even try. I have seen that look before. Had it myself once or twice. In the morning he came early with his wagon stacked with a lot of things—shovels, picks, blankets, grub—and underneath I saw a new saddle and two brand new Winchesters tucked away.

He really wasn't trying to hide them from me so I did not say anything. He just handed me the keys and we shook hands. I wished him good luck and he rolled out on me without looking back.

Now I ain't no storekeep either. I just ain't one, so what happened next was good luck for me.

One afternoon, about three o'clock, a large freight wagon loaded with stuff pulled into town, pulled by two beautiful large mules. Behind came a surrey driven by a dusty lady with a sunbonnet and a smile. Her horse was a skinny, red, long-legged trotter with a piebald face and three white stockings, a fine animal. They came directly to my stable just glancing about as they passed through town.

The man jumped off his wagon with a huge smile on his

face, taking off his big straw hat as he came.

I looked him over good, like I always do. I'd say he was forty, in good shape, dressed in store-bought clothes that looked dirty but new. His boots were beauties—low range heels, pointed toes for fitting in a stirrup and thick bull-hide leather. He did not carry a gun. I did notice a double-barreled shotgun he left in his wagon boot with a holstered 44 hanging next to it. I wonder if he knew how to use them. I found out later that he did.

"My name is Benjamin Davey and that's my wife, Rose, in the surrey there," he said. I nodded my head to him and tipped my hat a little to the lady. He stuck out his hand and I shook it. I noticed how fine his fingers were—kind of soft—but his grip was strong and firm.

"I'm Marion Fitz," I said, offering nothing more.

"I ran into a fella named Bill Palmer over at Gillette. He said you had a mercantile store here you might want to sell. That so?" he asked.

I was thrilled right away. "That's so," I said. "Come over here and have a drink of the only decent water in these parts." I made a lot of friends with my water. He grinned from ear to ear and I liked him. He pumped up a big dipper full of water, letting it overflow until it was all clear and cool and rather than taking a drink himself, he carried it over for his wife. I thought that was right nice. She drank the whole thing while he waited, asked her if she wanted more. She first shook her head, taking her sunbonnet off and tossing her yellow hair about her shoulders. I saw then how pretty her face was and how pleasant her smile. Mr. Davey pumped his own dipper of water. I just couldn't help looking back at her.

"The store, Mr. Fitz, is the one I passed coming in on the right next to a hotel, I believe?"

"Ain't always a hotel, as such, but passes as one if you don't mind—the other. Anyhow, it's the only one in this town and, anyhow, that's it all right."

"Could use some paint."

"Yep—could."

"You got a price?"

"Nope, you go look it all over and make me an offer. All of it—lock, stock and cracker barrel."

"Will you take care of our stock while we get checked in at the hotel?"

"Tell you what. Let's assume we are going to make a deal. There is a nice living quarters above the store with a stove, bed and all. It's very clean. And everything in it has been washed and cleaned good, including the bedclothes. It even has one of those new-fangled indoor flush toilets, would you believe? Move in there and we will talk in the morning."

"That couldn't be better for us, sir. We are obliged and give you our thanks."

Like I said, I liked him. Talked sort of funny, like Easterners. I went and got the keys for him. When I came back, he was talking quiet-like with his wife and they were both smiling big.

"Mr. Fitz," she said. "Is there a bathtub in the place there?"

"No, Ma'am." I answered. "There is a place for one and even a water pump for it, but Bill never got around to putting one in. He always took his bath at the barbershop. 'Luckey's Salon,' he calls it. It's just a barbershop with a nice bathtub and sprinkle shower behind the chairs."

"Thank you. I will go inquire," she said. "I need a bath."

Oh my. It was interesting what went on from there.

They left with a wave and in a little while Ben (I learned to call him Ben) came back sitting on the horse and leading the mules. He turned them over to me in the corral where they were watered, rubbed and fed before Ben went back.

I know what happened in detail. Rose put her stuff away

and carrying clean clothes and a towel, saunters over to the barber's salon where she asks for a bath. Luckey certainly agrees and leads her in back of the barbershop through the curtain where a bath was all set up and ready.

"Everything you need is here," and, looking back, he says, "In here is some special lavender-perfumed yucca shampoo, just for you. I'll just close the curtains and stand by the front door so no one comes in. Have yourself a nice bath, as long as you want."

But—there was a backdoor. Luckey said later it just slipped his mind. Also must of slipped his mind that the bath was all set up for Martin who always walked across the alley through the back door. Must of slipped his mind. Rose's body was sitting down low in the tub, all covered with the yucca suds, when open goes the back door and Martin comes in sort of backwards—stripping off his shirt and undoing his britches. She lets out a little squeak and when Martin turned around, his eyes liked to bug clean out of his head. He just stood there for a second holding his shirt in front of him with the big shiny star catching the light.

"I don't think there is room for two of us in this tub," she says.

"Oh, Ma'am. I am sorry. Pardon me—OK—pardon me. I should have knocked but I never—oh, excuse me!"

He turned to go out quickly. "Oh, sheriff, would you please dump that bucket of water on my hair for me. I really cannot reach it."

"Oh yes, ma'am, yes ma'am."

He grabs the bucket and dumps it over her head as she rinses out her hair.

"Thank you. You can go now if you will," she starts to stand up and Martin gets himself out of there in a hurry through the curtains and out the front door. They could hear her giggle outside where some guys were lounging on the boardwalk porch. Man, they were grinning wide.

"No one better laugh," spits out Martin.

No one did, but they sure did grin. I saw Martin as he crossed the street to the saloon. Man, I want to tell you. He sure as hell was grinning, too!

7

Next morning George was over to my stable looking after his horse when the Daveys came over, both of them, walking business-like.

"Howdy-do this morning," I said. "The place OK?"

"Yes, very good," they both chimed.

They both glanced over where George Martin was standing with a bucket of grain in his hands looking at his shoes. I mean looking only at his shoes.

"This here is Mr. Ben Davey, George, and his wife Rose. George Martin, town constable."

"How do you do, sir?" says Ben coming over to shake hands.

"We have met," said Rose, with just a hint of a smile.

George shook hands with Ben friendly-like, then damn if he didn't stick his big paw out to shake hands with her. His eyes never left her eyes and it was hers that looked down as they shook. Her whole hand disappeared in his paw. I couldn't help notice how gentle he was.

Ben looked at them puzzled but didn't say anything. After, we kicked dirt and talked about the weather a while.

"You got an offer for me?" I asked finally.

"Yes, I do. We do not want to buy the building. When the railroad comes in here it will be too small."

"Oh," I said, disappointed.

"We have a better offer, Marion."

"Call me Buck."

"We have a good deal for the both of us. I think you will

agree. How about we buy all the material and things in there for five hundred dollars and rent the building for thirty dollars a month?"

I really ain't no businessman, but I was relieved plenty. "Five hundred dollars for the merchandise and $50 for rent," I said it kind of halfheartedly, I knew.

"Done!" he said. I ain't no storekeep.

"Good," says Ben as he reached into a money belt under his shirt. He handed me $500 in greenback hundreds. I noticed there was another one left in the wallet. He reached into a front pocket and handed me two twenty-dollar gold pieces. "Rent begins on the first of the month, all right?"

I was pretty giddy. "Yes, yes, sure, all right." It was only the tenth which means he gets twenty days free. That was fair I guessed and we shook hands all around with pleasant looks. I could have got $600. I should have got $60.

8

Rose and Big George had an attraction to each other. It was obvious and any fool could see it. They exchanged glances and looks at each other when there was no reason. They looked away from each other at other times when maybe they should have been looking toward each other. George smiled too much around her and Rose smiled back, always with a knowing look. I saw him reach and take her hand when they met on the street and hold it for a slight squeeze, then let go like he really did not want to let go. Their eyes met at such times and the look of some longing was on each. It wasn't that she was a flirtatious woman. There was a reluctance there, held her back some.

So I noticed. I wondered if Ben ever noticed. I really did not know if he did. It didn't show. They passed each other on the street. They ran into each other in the café. George was in their store too much, usually while Ben was working in the back. Once I saw him kiss her on the forehead holding her two hands between them. I noticed that she closed her eyes while he did. I saw it through the window and they knew I saw them. I was going to go into the store, but I turned and walked away.

None of my business, I thought. *Be careful, George. Be careful, Rose.* It all worried me.

Ben was a good man. A real good man. One time I was in his new store having a smoke and a Mexican guy came in. His name was Pablo. He was a fine guy who always had a big shiny smile on his face. He had a small farm and ranch down by the river where he scraped out a living for his wife and four or five kids. He had brought a big sack of pinto beans and asked if Ben would trade for flour and lard. He did not speak English well and was greatly surprised when Ben answered him in good Spanish. He smiled all the more and it was a good thing to see. Now, I knew that Ben did not particularly want those beans. I saw him looking at his wife and kids sitting outside on the buckboard. They looked a little hungry to me. Ben lifted up the sack of beans and held them like he was weighing them, then handed Pablo a ten-pound sack of white flour and while Pablo was grinning, he stuck another ten-pound sack of cornmeal under his other arm.

"Oh no, señor. Too much. I ask for nothing but a fair trade."

"Fair trade is what I say it is," said Ben. "Come on."

Ben picked up a tin of lard and motioned him toward the door. On the way he grabbed a big jar of peppermint candy sticks and urged Pablo out the door.

"You make tortillas?"

"Si."

"You make me some, huh?"

"OK, señor.

"Fair trade is you bring me some white flour ones and some cornmeal ones. OK? Fair trade?"

"I bring you as many as you want. You never run out."

Ben went outside with him, put the lard in the back of the wagon, then opened up the candy jar. Little brown hands reached for them eagerly while they flashed white toothy smiles.

Ben watched them pull away and grinned and waved. He said a lot of things in Spanish that I didn't quite catch. They answered also as they looked and waved back.

When Ben came back inside, his smile faded.

“I hate tortillas,” he said as he busied himself behind the counter again.

Yes. He was a good man so I wondered and fretted about George and Rose. She was such a pretty woman and he—he was a plain guy, older, with a big nose.

9

One late morning Rose came over to the stable. She was wearing riding britches, a loose fluffy blue blouse and her hair was held up in a red bandana. I could see she had light rouge on her cheeks and on her lips. God, she was pretty.

"Saddle my horse for me, will you, please, Mr. Fitz? I would like to go for a ride."

"Certainly, Ms. Rose. My pleasure. Where you going?"

"Up the river, I guess

"Good. There are trees there and it is fairly shady."

When he was ready, she climbed on the big red without help and smiled. "Watch out for snakes," I said.

She glanced back at me without answering and waved her hand in a way that put me in my place.

Now, wouldn't you know, George Martin wandered over trying to act casual. "Howdy, Buck."

"Howdy, sheriff." I just stood there wondering.

"Is my horse in the stall? I think I'll take a ride."

"Along the river?" I asked.

"Yeah, guess so."

He went and saddled up inside the barn, then came out leading his mount. "Adios," I said from my work at the anvil. "Watch out for snakes."

He looked at me curiously, mounted up, and rode away at a fast trot.

It was a beautiful day, very warm but not yet too hot. The blue skies had puffs and feathers of white clouds holding perfectly still. The smell of the trees, bushes and grasses filled the air with an unmistakable scent. A family of quail exploded out of the bush startling the horse for just a minute.

Rose spoke to him in a whisper and patted his neck until he was calm and deliberate again. Songbirds were busy in the trees and hopping on the ground and there were mockingbirds, great-tailed grackles and finches. In the wet areas along the river where cattails grew, she saw red-wing blackbirds. She found herself studying the ground looking for snakes. When she realized what she was doing, she giggled at herself. She unbuttoned the front of her blouse when she felt a little breeze come up. She felt its cooling touch between her breasts and soon she pulled her blouse out of her britches all around and let her shirttails hang. She wore a half camisole that left her stomach bare as well. It was nice to be cool and comfortable.

She rounded a bend in the road then followed a nice trail down to the edge of the river where grass grew to the water. The river, slowed by the turn, became a slow-moving pool sparkling in the sunlight and shadows against the wall of red and orange rocks on the other side.

Rose stopped her horse and just sat looking, aware of the peaceful, colorful beauty before her.

She heard the soft hoof-steps of the horse coming behind her and saw the tall Texas hat above the bushes before he turned enough to appear at her side. Their eyes met and they each brought a soft smile across their faces.

Without a word, the big man also sat and viewed the scene for a little while before dismounting and giving Rose a hand as she slid from her mount. George picketed the horses where very soon they were busy chomping grass.

George unrolled a thick blanket and laid it out on the soft grass after getting a few rocks out of the way.

Rose sat down with George beside her. Soon her left

hand was wrapped safely in his. George felt her presence, her force, her life in his hand filling his own being. He took off his hat ceremoniously, looked hard into her eyes, then bent over very gently and found her soft full lips with his. Her arms came around his neck as she lay back on the blanket. She was aware then that her blouse was open and his hand was on the bare skin of her abdomen moving gently up as he pushed the loose camisole up, releasing her full breasts. The soft pink nipples became firm and inviting, sensitive, tingling with anticipation as he kissed and caressed. She pulled at his shirt wanting to feel his bare chest on hers.

"My god, you are beautiful. I love you, Rose. I love you."

"I want you," she murmured.

They made love then, soft, gentle and long, in the sunshine and shadows.

They lay together for a while, not talking at all. George tried to kiss her and she began a playful little giggle.

"You know what, cowboy?"

"What?"

"We should go for a swim."

She got quickly to her feet, pulling him along after. They ran the few steps to the bank and jumped in. She laughed and sang as she splashed him from top to bottom.

"Better than a bathtub," she giggled.

He played like he was helpless, covering his face, crying out for mercy. Her laughter was good and so was his. Suddenly he turned toward her, creating great splashes that soon had her in full retreat as she dove into the water and swam out to the middle of the pool. They swam there together for a while, touching arms and shoulders and hands and heads. He tried to kiss her under water but she playfully pushed him away and he came up coughing. Laughter, fun and love filled the air.

When they came out of the pool, they sat on the blanket until the sun dried them, sitting side by side with his arms around her and her head on his shoulder. They got dressed again, slowly, and parted after long kisses.

"I love you, Rose."

"Thank you for loving me."

10

It was early evening when they came back, riding together now. I came up and took her horse by the reins and would have helped her down except she threw one leg over the saddle horn and just hopped down. I noticed things, her clothes were kind of wrinkled. The bandana was off her hair and her hair fell down around her shoulders. I could not help notice that her hair was wet. I mean really wet. Not like sweat.

Ain't none of my business, I thought.

She walked over to town, not looking back. Big George just unsaddled his horse, put him away and wandered off hardly saying good-bye.

"Ain't none of my business," I said out loud.

The next day, Ben was leaving for Phoenix by way of Gillette to pick up a lot of merchandise for his store. He would be gone a week or more. It was a rough road to Gillette and the river not so bad from there. There were a lot of road bandits there and it worried me some. When I told him this as he was crawling on his empty wagon, he showed me a big double-barrel shotgun down in his wagon boot, as well as the damnedest big pistol I had ever seen. It had a twelve-inch barrel, I swear.

"My Buntline," he said. His mules were eager to get moving and in fine shape. He clicked his tongue at them and off they went down the road at a goodly pace.

I wonder if he kissed his wife good-bye, I thought to myself.

Now, I don't spy on people. Ain't my nature or my intention.

That night, right after sundown, I was walking down the alley behind the store heading for the saloon. The lantern was lit in the apartment above the store where Rose and Ben lived. No, I couldn't help seeing through the window into the room. I wasn't spying. I just couldn't help seeing. Rose was standing there looking toward the door at someone coming in. I guess I knew who. They stood there together, kissing for a long time. Then she blew out the lantern and it was dark.

Be careful, George. Be careful, Rose. Be careful.

Somehow it made me melancholy-like and I wished I had not seen anything at all. I went over to the saloon and drank too much beer.

11

Ben had gone into Phoenix without a hitch. He found his merchandise that he got for a good price. They loaded it on his wagon for him and although it was heavy, not too heavy for his mules, they were prime. He left Phoenix early in the morning and made it to Gillette at dusk—a little less than halfway home. He stayed at the hotel in Gillette, got up very early and was on the road before sunrise.

The day was hot as usual and the road was dusty. He had a large jug of water with him on the seat and took frequent swallows because he knew how fast a man could get all dried out and sun sick. The mules plodded along peacefully. The trail was flat with no pull for them. Ben was humming a little tune to himself watching the desert scenery go by. For some reason he looked back over his shoulder behind him when he saw the dust trail of horses off to the side of the road. They were obviously headed toward him. Why not on the road? *They are trying to stay out of sight,* he thought. He watched them getting closer, veering away to the side of the road staying parallel to it.

Ben looked up ahead. There was a sharp bend in the road with Palo Verde trees and large Greasewood trees just up ahead. He slid off the seat behind the wagon boot with just his eyes looking over the guard board. He took his hat off, sat the jug of water on the floorboard and reached for his double-barrel 12-gauge loaded with heavy buckshot. He put the shotgun in a position of rest then laid his buntline by his side on the floor.

They will jump me as soon as I go around the corner, he thought.

He crouched down more, fingered his double-triggers, made sure the safety was off and got ready to shoot.

He was right. There were three of them and they thundered out of the brush with the pistols in their hands. Ben cut loose. He hit the first man full in the upper throat and face, blowing him from the saddle. In an instant, he cut loose on the second man in the same way, making short work of him. The third man's horse was spooked and dancing around, but he managed to get a shot off with his rifle before Ben pulled down on him with the pistol. Two shots. Ben could hear the bullets splat home. The man slumped over in his saddle trying to raise his rifle up. Ben took a second to sight-down the barrel, squeezed off and could see where the bullet smashed into the side of his chest. Somehow he was draped over the saddle horn hanging on the mane as his horse darted off with the other two riderless horses.

"I hope you die fast," Ben yelled after him. Ben had gotten a good look at him.

"He is just a damned baby face boy!" Ben said aloud to himself. "A west Texas wild one."

It was then Ben started to feel the searing pain in his left thigh. The bullet from the boy's rifle had gonc through the driver box and ripped into his thigh. There was a large spot of blood filling his pant leg. Ben tore the cloth away from the entrance hole and looked. Wood splinters were sticking out of a gaping hole. There was a lot of oozing but no heavy bleeding. He gritted his teeth and pulled out the splinters as best he could. This caused more bleeding, so he took his large bandana from around his neck and another from his pocket and wrapped them lightly around the wounded leg. He felt dizzy and sick and in pain.

His mules had stood quietly through this after their initial startled jumps and awaited his orders. He gave them a "giddy up" and they started off as if nothing had happened.

"My god," said Ben out loud. "It is two days back from here." He thought of returning to Gillette but dismissed the idea. There was no doctor there, no one to look after him or his merchandise. If, a big if, he were to get out of there alive he would have nothing left.

"Follow the road boys, just follow the road. Skip along or I'm gonna die. I might die anyway."

But he didn't. He kept the mules going night and day with only short rests. He drank his water and ate soda biscuits and dried beef when he could. His leg hurt something terrible, but he managed to stop the bleeding with a light bandage made from the two of his bandanas tied together.

It throbbed and ached and hurt like hell, with every jar in the road cutting into him like burning-hot pokers. If you asked him how he got back to Sweetwater, he would just shrug his shoulders and say, "Damned if I know, damn good mules." He sure was fond of them mules.

I went to the stable just at daybreak. There was his wagon, with his mules just stomping the ground every now and then, but mostly just standing with their tired heads hanging down as far as they could go.

I found Ben near passed out in the boot, kind of under the seat, I ran and got water and he eagerly gulped two pitchers before I made him hold up.

"I've been shot in my left thigh. Hurts like it is on fire. Can't get up."

I got a saddle blanket, wadded it up under his head and laid him on his side and ran to get him another drink.

"Best drink of water I ever had." He tried to smile but it didn't work.

I ran into town as fast as my old bowlegs would let me to get help.

Big George and the Mexican were on the street.

"Ben has been bad hurt. Shot in the leg. He needs help now."

Without a word they high-tailed over to my place. George looked over the boot at Ben. He was ghostly white and his thigh was covered with a sticky maze of coagulated blood caked around the bandana bandage.

"What happened, Ben?"

"I got bushwhacked by three hombres a half-day out of Gillette. One got me right through the side of the box here. Got my thigh."

He pointed to a large rifle hole blasted through the plank. "I couldn't get all the splinters out without more bleeding. Just wrapped it. God it hurt like holy hell."

"Let's get him over to Doc's old office. Lead the team alongside his door in front there," George ordered.

George bent over the wagon and lifted out the 12-gauge shotgun, opened it and looked at the empty belly. He glanced at Ben with a question on his face. Instead of saying anything he reached under the seat and brought out the buntline pistol. He checked the cylinder and noted the three shots that had been fired.

"Where are the guys?"

"Buzzard bait," Ben croaked. "About five miles the other side of the river crossing."

"You got all three?" George asked with respect in his tone.

"Yup," says Ben. "I got 'em, but they shot me. It hurts man. God, I am thirsty."

"Let's get him over to the Doctor's place," he ordered.

We led the team and wagon up to the doctor's door and when it was open, big George reached in the wagon.

"Put your arms around my neck and hold on. This will hurt for a minute."

With this the big man carried him in and laid him on the examining table. Ben gritted his teeth. I knew he wanted to scream but only a soft moan escaped his clenched lips.

"Get Frances, will you Paco? Tell her I need a lot of boiling water, some towels, and a clean sheet or something."

Paco beat feet out the door heading across the street to the café

"Someone should get Rose," I said without looking at him.

"Yeah—Yeah," says George. "We will send Paco when he gets back with Frances. Let's see what the hell we got here."

George found a big pair of scissors and cut the bandage and pants leg away. I am telling you I never saw anything like it. The thigh was swollen up twice its size, black, blue, red and shiny like a huge eggplant. The entrance wound was jagged, black around the edges and seeping blood-singed serum. We took the rest of his clothes off, cutting them away so we wouldn't have to jar him as much and covered him with a flannel blanket we found in the cupboard. I had put a bucket of water in the wagon so I brought it in, soaked up some guaze and laid them on his chest, face and forehead. He was so hot, they seemed to dry right away. George was looking through drawers and cupboards. He found a bottle labeled LAUDANUM (OPIUM).

He raised Ben's head some and had him suck down a few swallows.

"Not too much, Ben. This will help the pain."

Frances came stomping in with her apron still on and looked over the scene. She had a large teakettle of hot water in one hand and towels stuffed under her other arm. "Let me see," she said as she pulled off the blanket covering his leg. Her mouth came open with a quiet gasp.

"Got trouble. There is festering. Lots of crap in that

hole—wood, dirt, cloth. It has to be opened up so we can clean it and it can drain. You up to it, Sheriff? We can't do it without some ether. The pain would kill him by itself." Without answering, she dropped the blanket and went across the room and opened a box. Inside was an ether mask and three cans of ether.

"Enough to put a horse out," she said.

"Do you know how, Frances?"

"I do. I helped Doc many a time in here."

Preparation was then made by finding surgical knives, clamps, scissors and forceps. We laid them all on a towel while Frances scalded them over and over on both sides. In the meantime, Paco had been sent for Rose and to boil more water at the café. Rose came in with a look I can best call as brave and worried. She went right over to Ben, took his cheeks in her hands and whispered to him. He was all groggy from the opium stuff but opened his eyes and even smiled. Odd, I heard him say, "Thank you" before he drifted off again.

Paco brought more hot water and set it down to cool some.

"Wash your hands, Doctor George. You got work to do." George took off his shirt and washed his hands over and over with the soap he found.

"I guess I am ready," he said as he looked over the doctor's tools. Frances looked hard at Rose. "Let's go then. Step aside, honey. Go sit over there. Paco and Marion, hold his arms and legs. They like to toss around a lot."

We took hold, Rose went and sat down obediently, looking awful pale. George and Rose didn't look at each other. Frances put the mask over his nose and mouth and began dripping the ether slowly and continuously. Ben got all restless and tried to struggle but we held on tight. After a while, his breathing got real deep and loud and he quit coughing from the fumes. He felt limp as a ragdoll.

"You ready, Doc?" asked Frances. "As soon as his eyes stop going from side to side, you get on with it."

George perched over his thigh.

"Time," said Frances.

First George had me wash his thigh and crotch with lye soap, then rinse it with warm water. George stepped up and took the knife in his hands. He cut away all the black skin all around the wound down to pink, twitching muscle. He pulled out pieces of wood splinters and pieces of cloth from his pants leg using the scissors and forceps. He could feel the hard fibro band that covers the muscle on the outside of the leg. It was tense. Using the scissors he cut up and down. All kinds of things I have seen and smelled, but nothing like this. Out it spewed with a gush, old blood, serum and pus.

"Get the teakettle there, Buck. While I hold it open, you wash it all out. Go ahead, pour it in."

I did.

George splashed the water around and dug in with his fingers pushing out some clots and dead muscle while I rinsed away the stuff. He felt around with his long fingers and pulled out a flattened bullet and tossed it on the floor.

"I can feel the bone. It is not broken."

We washed and rinsed with all the water we had and everything looked pink and clean. Some bleeding places. He continued with the heated red-hot knife under an alcohol flame burner.

"Almost out of this can of ether. I have to let him wake up soon," said Frances. "Paco, you fetch that sack of moldy bread from my kitchen. Right by the stove."

"What do I do with that?" George asked.

"Pack that hole with the moldiest greenest piece you can. Shake the mold all in there."

That he did when Paco brought it over. Then I held his

leg up by the heel and George covered the thigh with a lot of loose rags and towels and held them with strips of sheets tied loosely around the leg.

He woke up pretty quick tossing and turning some so we had to hold him until he was quiet. We turned down the cot in the corner of the room, washed the gore off his naked body, dried him all off. Then George picked him up like a child and laid him on the sheet. Frances had us keep him awake to be sure he could breathe good. Then we covered his chest and belly with cold wet towels. In just a short time he began sleeping peaceful-like.

Rose still sat in her chair across the room, her face shiny wet with tears. She seemed to be sobbing but made no sound. Frances went to her, took her hands and led her over to Ben. She knelt on the floor beside him, then cried for all she was worth.

Paco and I cleaned the place up while Frances and George talked quietly to each other away from the bed where Ben lay with his wife's head resting on his chest.

"You did a fine job, Martin. No one could have done better. He has a real good chance. I know," she added.

"What do we do now?" he asked quietly.

"Change those bandages a couple of times a day. I will try to keep you supplied with moldy bread. Keep as much mold in there as you can. Brown the towels in the oven to put right over the wound. The powdery stuff clots when it needs to and they will be clean. Wrap it loose so it can drain and—pray for him."

All that night, afternoon, and night again, Rose stayed with him talking quietly to him and holding his cheeks. She changed the wet towels over his chest and belly when they warmed up from his fever.

As soon as he could refuse, Ben would not accept anymore laudanum. He was hot and dry with fever that did not seem to break for days. George came twice a day and changed the bandages. I was surprised to see how gentle he could be. I wondered, you know, what Rose thought and felt about George too. The only words I heard between them was all business-like.

Paco was attentive and helpful. He brought in a small flask of brownish liquid. He told us that it was made from willow bark and that it would make the fever go down and the man sweat. Man did it ever! I couldn't believe that anyone could sweat so much. The fever came down on the fourth day and stayed down. That morning Ben sat up and told us that he was starving. Damned if I didn't get all worked up and had to sneak out. He was going to live.

In a week Ben was up walking around with a crutch. He still had a big bandage because his wound still leaked some. It was healing from the inside out as it should. He slit up the side of his pants leg then, pinned it together over the bandage. He liked to unpin it and show the kids when they came around to stare at him. It was funny to see.

Folks said that George saved his life. The big man said that Frances did it with her moldy-bread poultices. Frances thought that Paco's brown piss was the big factor. The truth was they all had a hand in it and the mules. Them mules brought him right home when he was about passed-out cold. Ben came out every day to see them and talk to them. He brushed them until they were shiny, fed them extra corn and oats. He was right fond of them animals.

12

Things were quiet again for a little while anyway. Martin sent a letter to the governor of the territory inquiring about being appointed Federal Marshall. I thought he would get it all right. No one else wanted the job—low pay—danger—hot, dusty lonesome trails. Also, he spent hours studying law books and he intended to be a legal lawyer in a couple of years at most.

Him and Rose never saw each other much as far as I know anyways. I noticed they never looked at each other long but I caught a far away longing in both their eyes from time to time and George was too damn quiet. Time to do something.

"George, let's go hunting. There are some deer down by the river. Frances wants some meat."

His eyes perked up and smiled at last.

"Yeah, let's do it. Can you hit anything?"

"You will be surprised," I said.

A couple of days later we were up way before dawn; saddled up with pack horses all rigged and on the trail toward the river before the sun started painting the clouds orange. A light warm breeze was blowing gently in our faces as we walked and trotted quickly along.

When we got to the river breaks where the brush grew green between the cottonwoods and Palo Verde trees, we picketed the horses, grabbed our rifles and after changing our boots for moccasins, crept toward the river. As we got closer, we walked slow and quiet, me in front with the breeze to our faces so anything down there would not catch our scent.

Mule deer can hear, God knows, but they can smell too. There is no sneaking up on them at all. You have to find a place you can watch kind of hidden too. We found a place with a good view of an open space below so I left George there and crept up-wind looking for another. Out of the corner of my eye I caught a movement about fifty yards down near an open meadow. I pulled back and waited behind a tree. Three big does tippy-toed out in the clearing with three smaller deer behind them. Last spring's fawns. They were heading in George's direction. Although I had a perfect shot, I wanted George to get the meat so I waited and watched their tails disappear in the brush leading toward his meadow. Then, darn, I caught sight of a huge cat sniffing along the deer's trail. It was bright yellow, sleek and prime and pretty. I just watched it walk slowly and silently after the deer with his long tail wagging from side to side like a snake until it too disappeared into the brush. I turned and made my way back to where George was sitting under a tree. I motioned for him not to move and be quiet. We both looked intensely down on the open space waiting.

The deer stepped out slowly as before, sniffing the breeze, stopping and loitering. Looking all around. Soon they started munching on the small weeds between the grass. George raised his rifle to take aim at the big lead doe. It would be fine eating all right. I laid my hand on his arm and shook my head. He looked puzzled as he lowered his rifle. I pointed to the small trail the deer had come down. Soon the big cat appeared like a yellow shadow. One instant there was nothing, then it appeared. It crouched low, pushing one foot at a time slowly, slowly before him until he was on the edge of the clearing, not thirty feet from the deer. He hunched himself back ready to spring, his tail went still. I nudged George and he brought his rifle up and fired off just as the puma launched himself. It was a good shot and the puma dropped like a sack of wood. I had been ready to back him up. When I knew he had hit, I swung my little carbine over and nailed the big doe before it could run off. It was a hell of a shot, if I do say so myself.

We stood up, slapped each other on the back, grinning and laughing.

"I'll be damned!" said George. "I'll be!"

We tumbled down the incline not too gracefully and proceeded to look over the puma. He was a big tom—the largest I have ever seen or heard of. His body alone was five feet. His tail another three. He had black around his eyes and mouth, with gray in his cheeks around his whiskers. His coat was shiny and soft. You could see the outlines of his smooth muscles. Although he was fat, he was firm and you could feel his strength, picture his sleek speed and agility. Looking at his face revealed his intelligence, skill and stealth.

"This here is one of the finest animals God ever made," I whispered.

"Kind of a shame," George said softly.

"Naw. Look at this. He is in good shape now, but he would never make the winter. He is old, that's why he is so big."

I pulled his lips back and we saw his teeth were all worn down and one had a big purple-red abscess cooking under it.

"Pretty soon he wouldn't be able to eat and the infection would get him. I have seen it before. Their teeth go, then they go. In a way you did it a favor."

"Heck!" muttered the big man. "I don't think he would look at it that way."

"Get to skinning. The hide comes off a lot easier while they are still warm. Leave the head attached for now. You know what? Old hunters and trappers say cougar is the best eating of all. Never tried it, but I guess we will now. I will need some help rolling the doe over."

"What doe?" says George, all quizzical.

I pointed over on the edge of the brush. He was so up in the air shooting the cat he had not even noticed my carbine go off. We walked over to look at it. I had hit it right in the spine at the back of the neck at the withers. Like I said, it was a hell of a shot. I am a hell of a shot!

"I'll be double damned!" says George, taking off his hat and wiping his brow with his bandana.

The fun's over, now the work begins. I cleaned the deer Mexican-style. That is, I skinned her, completely cut off her head and legs at the joints, hooked her rear legs through the space by her tendons, called George over and hung her up on a tree. Then I took my hatchet, opened her brisket, split her pelvis wide, then opened her with my knife, taking care not to poke into anything. It all comes out as one then from gullet to one with stomach, heart, liver and lungs still hooked together. I don't really like liver, but I like deer liver so I kept it aside as I threw the gut pile twenty feet away in the brush. I am fast. I had done this more than a few times before. I went over then to help George. He was doing a beautiful job, skinning out the paws and all around it neck up under the chin. We made quick work of it then, leaving the head and tail attached to the intact hide.

"I don't know about eating this cat," George mentioned.

"Well, me neither. I never ate a cat as far as I know."

We agreed to take the back strips, tenderloins and boned-out haunches and let the rest go. Later on when we ate them steaks, we wished we had kept it all. Best wild meat I ever ate.

I went and got the horses while he built a hat-sized fire, made a ring of rocks to make some coffee. We squatted down there in the grass feeling fine. I had brought some tortillas stuffed with shredded meat and beans with small mild-roasted chilies and onions. I brought out two cups made of fired clay to drink our coffee. George looked at them.

"Well, what?"

"I hate damn tin cups, too. You burn your hands and lips and can't even drink the stuff till it cools down."

"By god, you're right. Give me one of those."

We laughed and laughed and had a grand time all stuffed with good food and coffee that we could drink still hot. We leaned up against some cottonwoods and had us a smoke. It wasn't even 10 o'clock and still cool.

He was too quiet but a little restless. He looked off into the distance a lot, gazing at nothing.

"You troubled, George?"

"No, no—well, maybe a little."

"I know why, man."

"You do?" he asked.

"Yes." I paused a long time. "She is a fine and beautiful lady."

"I know." This time he paused a long time. "I love her," he said softly.

"George, she is not yours to love that way."

We paused there on the grass and just laid beside the river, smoking. George did not say anything but just looked like he was far away.

"Love is a powerful, confusing thing sometimes—all the time. You been in love before, George?"

"Yeah—yes, I have," he said after a pause.

"Been married?"

"Yes. Down in South Texas. I had a wife and daughter. We had a small ranch out a ways from McAllen. I had plans to make it a big ranch a little at a time. I was a Texas Ranger then, too, cause we needed the money—as little as it was."

"Tell me about her."

"Her name was Donna. She was about an eighth Mexican. She was a gentle, sweet person who was always doing something for someone else. Kind. Just kind. She was only twenty-four when she was killed."

George looked up to the sky at the treetops, the river, his feet—anywhere but at me.

"George, I know it ain't none of my business. I don't want to open old, healed-up wounds."

"I guess they never did heal all the way."

He glanced at me then looked quickly away.

"I want to tell you," he paused a long time looking straight ahead.

"Comancheros came through while I was on patrol away from home. Wild, crazy half-breed Mexican-Indian. They robbed, burned, rustled, destroyed, raped."

He hung his head down with his chin on his chest. Very quietly he said with a choke in his throat, "Raped and murdered women and children."

It was me that could not look at him then.

"I found out what happened before I came on home. The captain rode out and told me everything. My wife was gone. My six-year-old daughter was gone, my house and barn burned down, and my livestock killed or scattered."

He began to move about talking louder and faster. I noticed that his fist was clinched tight.

"I picked up their trail and followed it for weeks. I lost it a lot of times in the rocks but it was not that hard to follow. It was obvious when they turned back to Mexico. I rode night and day to get ahead of them where I knew they were going to cross the river into old Mexico. There was a narrow pass through the rooks. I figured they would head through there because it was miles around, otherwise. I had seen the pass another time, too. I watched a couple of banditos go through, while I could do nothing on the other side of the Rio Grande.

"This time though I rode right across. I hid my horses a

half-mile away in some mesquite. I took Palo Verde branches and brushed out my tracks. I climbed the rocks so I was above the pass. I got toward the other end and found a narrow spot barely wide enough for a horse. The rooks had been rubbed about smooth. There were a lot of large loose rocks above where I was. It was easy to fill the whole thing up head high. Nobody was going to go through there on or off a horse. At the opening I piled some rocks leaving me a slot for a clear view of the floor of the pass. Then I sat back and waited. They came after daylight the next day. There were eleven of them riding on worn-out horses. They stopped before crossing the river, looking up and down and behind them. Then charged across whooping, laughing and shouting. They thought they were all safe in old Mexico. They stopped again looking all around at the entrance of the pass, then came through single file. All of them. I had all of the sons of bitches.

"When they got to my wall, I jumped up with my fully-loaded Winchester 64 rifle and cut loose. I shot and didn't miss. I aimed at their balls, then their guts. I did not miss. When some of them got to their guns, I slipped into my protected place and finished them off one by one. The ones that screamed and begged, I kept until last. I cursed them. I cursed them over and over. Goddamn murderers—child killers—raping dogs—you arc all going to hell!

"When nothing was left moving I went down there. I felt nothing. Nothing. I was like a stone I was so full of anger and hate. But you know it began to melt. I felt the ice melt off of me. I felt strong. I felt like I could jump forty feet. Green things seemed greener. I could see every sparkle and crack in the rocks. I felt like I could touch the sky.

"I emptied their pockets, cutoff their fingers to get their rings off—if I had to. I didn't care. I put their gun belts over the saddles and the rifles in scabbards or tied behind. I made a long string of horses and walked out of there. I left the filthy sons of bitches where they laid for the coyotes and buzzards.

"When I rode into McAllen it must have been a hell of a sight. Captain came up to me with his thumbs in his belt.

" 'You got them?' he said.

" 'I got 'em.'

" 'How many for god's sake?'

" 'All of them. I got all of them.'

" 'Good,' was all he said, counting the horses and looking at me."

"What did you do then?" I asked George. "I know you could not have stayed long." He got up then, leaned against a cottonwood and built a smoke.

"Well, can't say I was worth much for a while. I sold the ranch what was left of it—the land—for a few hundred bucks. I tried to get drunk a couple of times but it was not in me to be drunk, let alone a drunk. I stayed in Rangers a while. We caught some boys rustling cattle early one afternoon. The other two rangers I was with headed them off and they ran right by me—twenty feet—three of them. Young men. I did not even yell at them. I drew my six-gun but I could not fire. I just could not. When the Rangers rode up to me, they looked puzzled and pissed."

"What happened? They got clean away."

"Nothing. Nothing happened."

"I explained to the captain as best I could that evening.

" 'I didn't want to kill anyone, Cap. They were just wild, young men.' I left it hanging.

" 'George,' he said, 'let me tell you something. You took an oath with me to uphold the law and protect people and their property because they cannot protect themselves. You have to be able to do your duty. Those young guys will get older. Then they will rob and kill. Your clear duty was to stop them. Guys like you and me, we are big and strong and tough. We have an obligation. Do you understand? Do you want to protect, defend and help?'

" 'Yes—I really do, and I understand.'

" 'What do you want to do, George?'

"I took off my badge and laid it on his desk. 'I think I'll go north to Arizona and be a sheriff in some small town that wants me.'

"He didn't say anything. Nothing. Nothing showed on his face.

" 'It is time to get out of this part of the country,' I added.

" 'Good, Cap said. 'That's good. You are a fine man and I hope to see you again someday. You had better practice with your pistol,' he said with a wide grin. 'The better you are the less you have to use them.' "

The big man looked at me and managed some kind of a half-assed self-conscious grin. When he was done with the story somehow I knew I had done him a favor by just listening.

Then we commenced to go home! Should have seen the rodeo we had trying to put that cat skin with the head attached on to that mule. Rubbed blood on the damn nag's nose and that didn't even help. We finally skinned the whole thing out and threw the skull away, off in the bushes. We still had to roll the hide in a blanket to fool that jug-headed mule.

George was all silent again all the way back. He was thinking about Rose. I could tell.

13

It was not even a week later when we heard the Stouffer brothers were back in town. I knew here comes trouble. George wrinkled up his brow, but did not say much.

"They say Rodney is fast as they come with that .44. How fast are you, Constable Martin?" I asked with good humor.

The big man took it seriously.

"I'm fast enough. Not the fastest you ever saw but I have a big advantage."

"What's that?" I had seen how fast he was.

"I shoot straight always. I hit what I am aiming at." He said seriously. "When the Cap down in McAllen told me to get better with my six-gun, I knew he was not just kidding. I started strolling out just at dark when the rabbits start to show up. I practiced until I could draw fast, shoot from the hip, and hit them every time. He was right about another thing. So far, I have never had to pull the trigger on another man." He paused. "So far."

He said it like he knew it was coming to an end. We both did.

It was just a few nights later when a cowboy raced into the office from the saloon. He looked wild-eyed and desperate.

"Give me my guns. I'll kill the son-of-a-bitch," he yelled.

George jumped to his feet.

"What are you talking about? No one carries weapons in this town but me and my deputy. What happened?"

The cowboy was almost bawling.

"That Dude guy. He killed Ritchey. Stabbed him right in the throat with a pigsticker from up his sleeve. Ritchey said he saw him deal from the bottom of the deck. Ritchey made a grab for the cards and Dude stabbed him. He is over there saying it was self-defense, but it weren't either. Ritchey was grabbing the cards and he was not armed. His pistol is that one in the box."

He pointed to a beat up old Colt that looked like it had been used for a hammer. "Sit down. What is your name?"

"Man! My name is Monte Clark. I'm with the Bar 2 outfit just out of town waiting to load our beeves."

"OK, Monte. You just sit there now. I am the law here and my deputy and I will go arrest him. I don't want you getting killed. You can come later, but you will leave your guns here,"

Monte sat looking angry and sad all at the same time.

Big George strapped on his six-gun, gabbed a familiar looking double-barreled shot gun that he loaded with buckshot, then looked over to me. "Cover my back, Buck. You never know with these snakes."

Monte tagged along behind as we walked over to the saloon, we didn't try to stop him. I stood just inside the swinging doors with my rifle in hand and my finger on the trigger. George and Monte walked across the floor to where a table was tipped over and a young cowboy lay in a big pool of blood. It was so quiet in there you could hear a frog fart.

Dude stood there looking cocky and unconcerned.

"You, Rodney and Hoss—step way back, Buck, if they make any unnecessary moves, shoot 'em." The two brothers stepped back to where I waved them with my rifle barrel. "It was self-defense, Sheriff," Dude said with defiance in his voice. "He made a grab at me."

"Bullshit!" yelled Monte. "I saw it all." He just

grabbed your crooked cards!"

George still did not say anything.

"I thought he had a gun," Dude sounded a little worried. "Maybe a knife, I didn't know. I feared for my life. A man has a right to protect himself."

No one around the room said anything. I wondered what the Stouffer boys had said to them.

"He was unarmed. Do you see anything in that holster? His pistol is in my office. You know you are not to carry a knife in this town. I took it away from you before, so I know that was clear. You are nothing but a shit-hole, a tinhorn ass-hole, and you are under arrest for murdering an unarmed man as well as carrying a concealed knife. I will check those cards, too. My guess is they are marked. I should have slit your ugly throat when I took your knife before. Turn around."

He just stood there with a sneer looking over at his brothers. I waved my gun barrel a little in their direction and they did not move a muscle.

"Turn around," George said quietly.

This time Dude did as he was told. George grabbed his wrists and clamped on the handcuffs as tight as he could, making Dude wince and cry out loud.

"You are going to hang, asshole."

"Nobody is going to hang our brother," Rodney yelled.

"Oh yeah, shitface," the big man said. "You just wait and see."

"We will be coming after him!"

With this George pushed Dude along and out the door. I stood guard there until I knew he had plenty of time to get him to jail.

"Nobody move," I said as I backed out the door. I made a big show of cocking my rifle. Nobody moved.

George stood at the jail looking out the window with the

shotgun still in his hands. Dude still had the handcuffs on, even though he was locked in the cell.

"Get these damn things off me. They are cutting off my circulation. I can't feel my fingers."

"Shut your damn mouth. They are never coming off until after you hang." He did not even turn around.

"You will cripple my hands!" He sounded like he wanted to cry.

"You will never hang me you two-bit law dogs. My brothers are coming for you."

George turned and faced him. "If they come unannounced, these first two barrels are for you."

Dude looked scared as hell as he went over and sat on his bunk. "I have to piss," he said.

"Piss in your pants, Dude, cause those cuffs aren't coming off."

Dude just sat there. "I can't move my fingers," he whimpered.

It wasn't long. A couple of hours, Rodney called out from the street in front of the jail.

"I'm calling you out, Sheriff. Just you and me in this here street. Gun to gun. You man enough, you four-eyed law dog? Or do I have to come in there to get you?"

"Don't try to come in here, Rod," Dude yelled out the window. "Don't. They will kill me right off if you do."

"That's right, Stouffer. Take one step toward the jail and I blow his head off. Then we talk some more. How stupid *are* you, polecat?"

"Come out then, Sheriff, or everyone in the territory will know you are a chicken-shit coward."

"Where is your brother then?"

"He is watching the saloon."

"Watching the saloon, bullshit!"

"He is out there," George said to me. "I need you to

watch my back." After a pause George turned to me.

"I guess it is time," he said with resolve. "Gag that squeaking rock of shit there in the cell."

I did not even open the cell but made him stand with his face through the bars. "Open your mouth."

"Go to hell."

"No, you are the one going to hell." I stomped with all my might on his foot. He opened his mouth then, I'll tell you. I stuffed my dirty bandana in there, then tied another around his head.

"He is gagged, Constable."

"Good."

Then he yelled to Rodney, "I am coming out, Rodney. You go over in front of the alley. I don't want any innocent people hit. The light from the bar across the street will be just right. Buck, go out the backdoor and around to the other side and cover my back. If Rodney gets me, kill him. Look for his brother. Kill him too. But, hold this miserable scum for the hangman."

I waited until he stepped out on the porch, then went out the back way. I found a spot behind a barrel at the edge of the alley where I could see. I was just getting kneeled down when it felt like lightning hit my head. I saw a flash of light, then darkness. I came to slowly and with a terrible pain in my head. I felt the back of my scalp with my fingers, coming away sticky with blood.

For a long time I couldn't get up. I just crawled around dazed. My rifle was gone. So was the pistol from my belt. I could hardly see, but I was aware that big Hoss was standing in the shadows ten feet in front of me. I just could not get stood up. I got to my hands and knees then toppled over. I had a view, through my swimming eyes, I will never forget. Rodney stood with his hands out and his legs apart. As George came closer, his hands inched toward his gun.

"That's close enough."

They both stood facing each other. Suddenly Rodney yelped, "Reach!"

Two guns went off at almost the same time. Maybe Rodney was a little faster, I guess. George clutched his side, and big Rodney sort of swayed back and forth then crumpled to the ground with a gasp. From where I was, I could see a large blotch of blood on his chest just under his chin. Rodney may have been faster all right, but George did not miss.

George's hand clutched his left side. His pistol had fallen from his fingers into the dust. What happened next went so fast I can't tell you. Hoss raised his ax-handle club and screamed bloody murder like an animal and stampeded toward the lawman. I tried to yell but nothing came out of my mouth. My God! I thought he was dead for sure. Then be damned if a man didn't jump out in front of him with a small two-barrel Derringer in his hand.

"Stop or I'll shoot!"

Hoss stopped only a few feet away. He lowered his club and, so doing, brought his hand to the handle of his six-gun. He drew and fired and before the smaller man dropped. He had given Hoss both barrels right in his ugly face. He actually raised a cloud of dust when he fell dead as a stump. Someway, I had gotten to my feet and to George's side.

He looked bewildered behind him. I could see him summing it all up and putting it together.

He went over to the man lying on his back just behind him.

"Ben! Ben!" George bent over and pulled up his shirt, then saw where the bullet had gone through his upper abdomen. "Oh no, Ben!" It slipped out of his mouth unconsciously, naturally. I was there with my hand on his shoulder and I swear I could feel his pain. I wish I could have taken some of it from him.

Ben opened his eyes and George looked into them.

"You saved my life, Ben."

"You saved mine once, but you can't this time, George," he said in a whisper. George put his ear to his lips.

"Take care of Rose," were the last words Ben ever whispered.

14

The funeral took place on a bright, clear, peaceful morning. I don't like funerals much. Probably because someday I will be the guest of honor at my own. This one, I wanted to go to. I wanted to pay my respects and I hoped that somehow he would be looking down and see me there wiping my eyes. The preacher did a fine job. I particularly remember how he said that heaven holds a special place for people who give their lives to save another. He called it the sure and certain truth and I believe it is.

Constable, Big George, Martin, looked worn, very troubled and sad. I really understood why—I mean all the whys.

Rose sat on a chair that someone had brought her. She did not sit long but stood up with everyone else. She held her chin up and looked everyone in the eye. She did not twist her hanky or stare at her shoes or bawl like a calf like some do. But now, you could tell that her heart was broken and despair itself was just under the surface.

Frances walked her home afterward. She did not want to ride in the undertaker's black carriage.

No one saw much of her for a couple of weeks. I heard she had sold out her business for a good price and was fixin' to leave town for Phoenix. For a while I thought she was going to leave without saying goodbye to someone at all.

I was there when the stagecoach came through for her. Her big horse was tied on behind. Her boxes, trunks and suitcases were on top. George and I stood watchin' as they loaded up. Rose came out her door and walked right up to me first.

"Marion Fitz, you are a fine, honest man and I am proud to have known you. I want you to have the mules—Ben's mules."

I couldn't say a word except a croaked-out thank you. I think I did. I went to shake her hand, but she took both of mine and kissed me on both cheeks.

Then I stepped aside leaving her and George Martin facing each other. "I love you, Rose," I heard him whisper. "God, how I wish I could change things."

"No one can, cowboy," she said very kindly.

"Will I ever see you again? Can I? Will you let me someday?" She smiled through bright eyes sparkling with tears, "I will be in Phoenix waiting. You come when you see your way clear to do so." She took George's hands and held them to her chest to her heart.

"I will come when the time is right and I can," he said. "When I see my way clear."

"Soon?"

"Yes, soon."

Without a kiss—with only a look of love that could not be mistaken, she stepped into the stagecoach. It rolled out and was gone.

That was the longest day I ever remember in Sweetwater, Arizona, about 1886.

Part II

Trial at Sweetwater

1

Samuel Finn stood in the minimal shade of a short cottonwood tree beside his house on the edge of town. He was waiting not too patiently for Bobby to arrive with a load of wood for his stove. He pulled a pocket watch attached to a loop in his pants by a short chain made of pewter. He looked at his watch, twisted the knob on top, shook it vigorously then cursed softly.

"Damn thing doesn't work for a whit. Piece of junk!" he said.

He put it back in his pocket and squinted down the road at a mule-drawn wagon proceeding toward him, leaving a trail of dust as thick as smoke. It was piled high with wood, mostly branches in chunks and pieces of mesquite trees with the dried bark falling off. A dark-skinned, young man who appeared to be constantly smiling was driving the wagon. A closer look revealed a somewhat dull, distracted look on his face, which led one to know that he was at the best dull-witted. He wore overalls that were dirty and baggy with small rips and tears that were never repaired.

No one really knew where he came from. Some five years previously, he began living in an old shack down by the river with a couple of hound dogs and a good-looking mule that he called Roger and was obviously very fond of. He worked at odd jobs in town when he could. Shoveling out the stable, lifting and moving things for people, sweeping and cleaning and, in this case, bringing in firewood from the woods along the river. His dark skin, deep brown eyes and high cheekbones showed his Indian blood.

A breed he was called: half-Indian, half-Negro. People surmised that his father was probably one of the Texas cowboy's slaves before the war or were descendants of the slaves. His mother probably a Comanche, outcast from west Texas, that hung around the cow towns whoring for booze and a few dollars. Bobby never had a last name. He was pleasant, reliable and always friendly, lots of times too frequently friendly for comfort. Nonetheless, everyone knew him and treated him all right paying him fairly for his labors.

Sam was a prosperous store and pawnshop owner. He had few friends. None really, just acquaintances. He drove a hard bargain and his face always wore a scowl. His wife was an unhappy skinny woman, burnt black by the prairie sun and scarred by the ever-present blowing dust. It was said that she was touched. She died one winter night ten years before. Still a young woman at forty or so. Sam just walked into town and found the undertaker. There was no funeral of any kind. People were kind and respectful giving their condolences when they encountered him but no one went out of their way to look him up. Sam himself was pretty satisfied with himself. He had been over to the bank that morning and filled his billfold with a large amount of brand new five-dollar bills. He carried them in a billfold in a pocket that was inside his shirt next to his skin. He would pat it every now and then as if to ensure himself that it was still there.

He waved Bobby to alongside of his little clapboard house where Bobby came to a halt, pulling up the grateful mule. The dog sitting on the seat next to Bobby jumped down wagging his tail for all he was worth and ran right over to Sam with his long, red tongue ready to lap his hands with whatever he could reach with his lapper.

"Get outta here you," Sam said kicking at him.

The dog pulled his tail between his legs and looked

injured as he obediently retreated.

"Pile the wood right here alongside the house."

"Yes, sir, I will," said Bobby and he began immediately to unload and stack the wood while his mule simply hung his head and closed his eyes to sleep while the dog, whose name was Dog, went sniffing around the place making himself busy, slobbering and wagging his tail vigorously with the enthusiasm that only dogs possess.

Sam sat on his porch rocking in a Bentwood rocker that he had taken for pawn from some unfortunate immigrant and held his hand on his chest patting the precious billfold that was under his shirt. When Bobby had completed his task, he approached the boss man with his raggedy hat in his hands. "Ise done," he said. Sam stirred around and stood up facing him.

"Good, good, Bobby."

"You pay me now." It was a statement not really a demand and certainly not a question.

Sam had an instant idea. "Bobby I got something here for you, wait till you see." He undid the pocket watch and pulled it out of his pocket on the cheap chain with a flourish. "Tell you what I am gonna do, boy. I am gonna pay you with this fine watch. What do you think 'bout that?"

Bobby looked sad, "I need my two dollars," he replied flatly.

"Now, Bobby, can you tell time? Every man needs a watch don't you think? This is a fine watch for a load of wood."

"I can't tell time."

"You can learn can't you?" He patted the young man's shoulder as if to congratulate him already on his new watch.

"I don't know, I don't think I needs a watch."

'Sure ya do, boy," he said sternly, with anger in his voice and a vicious look on his face.

Bobby understood all right. He stood for a moment with disappointment painted on his shiny face then reached out slowly and took the watch, glanced at it then turned to leave. "I'm just throwin' in the chain," Sam said earnestly. Bobby said nothing else. He climbed into his now-empty wagon, called Dog aboard and plotted off in the direction that he had come. Sam went back to his seat, leaned back and lit a cigar. "Dumb half-breed son-of-a-bitch, can't even tell time."

Sam Fenton's house was right on the trail that led to the Aqua Frea River. Most days the Mexican women walked down to the river to wash clothes and to bring back water. Sam waited to see who would come by. Actually he was waiting to see if Rosa Rivas would come by. She was about sixteen and in her one-piece peasant's dress of cheap cotton looked wildly sexy to him. He could catch site of her slim brown legs from the knees down to her bare feet and he would be instantly aroused. With her hands holding the basket of clothes on her head, her dress bulged like ripe peaches, jiggling casually as she walked. Sam was thinking this over quietly in his mind when she came into view accompanied by her brother, a big boy of twelve named Paco. Sam could not take his eyes off of her as she came closer. He could feel the bulge as the blood rushed in. This excited him even more.

"She is ripe fer pickin' one of these days, one of these days," he panted. "Hell, today is a good day!" He jumped to his feet. "Hey, Rosa, Paka, come over here."

The pair looked at him and approached slowly and quizzically.

"Paco how would you like to earn a dollar?" He looked interested.

"Doin' what?" he asked.

"Cuttin' up these long branches so that they can fit into the stove, some of 'em are too damn long. Want to do that? I will give you a dollar."

"All right," said Paco. "I need an ax though. Mine has a broken handle on it.

"I have one around here," Sam said, taking his eyes off of Rosa for the first time. Paco noticed the way he looked at her and felt uneasy. Rosa didn't seem to notice as she turned with a soft adios and kept on toward the river. Sam found an old ax that was rusted and dull looking.

"It is dull and the handle is cracked," said Paco.

"I have a file in the house and we can wrap around the crack with rawhide," said Sam Fenton.

"OK," said Paco, "but that won't last."

"Well, boy, do what you can until I can git myself another."

Sam produced a file and some strips of rawhide and held the ax handle as Paco wrapped the handle around the split that was near the head. When this was done, he secured it with a knot and splashed water on the rawhide to make it shrink. Sam kept looking down the trail towards the river. He seemed eager and nervous. Paco noticed and was as uncomfortable as hell. Paco began sharpening the ax with the file and Sam took it as his chance to separate himself and strode casually down the trail towards the river.

He found himself walking faster and faster until he knew she was just in front of him. He went off the side of the road and into the bushes to wait. *She won't be long*, he thought as he took off his coat and unbuttoned his pants. Crouching like an animal he waited until he saw her coming up over the little hill up from the river. He stepped out in front of her suddenly. She knew immediately that there was trouble and, by the look on his face, she knew what kind of trouble. She took a step backwards, dropped the basket from her head and started to run. He grabbed her quick as a cat and threw the struggling girl on her back. Her exposed legs lit a fire in him and he reached up and slapped her hard on the cheek.

"Now don't make me do that again, you hear me. You are gonna like what's a comin' and it's comin' whether you like it or not."

She was stunned, frightened and crying as he climbed on her like an animal. He held both her hands with his left hand and began pulling her dress up with his right hand. He was shaking so much, he could hardly hold it in his trembling fingers. He reached for his belt, tugging it, and trying to unbutton his top button with a frenzy.

There was a blinding lightning bolt that crashed into the back of his head and neck. A big red bubble appeared behind his eyes, got bigger, then burst. Then nothingness; absolute blackness.

Later that afternoon Sheriff George Martin was sitting in his office reading his law books when two horsemen galloped up to his hitching rack, looped their reigns over the rail and stomped quickly into his office. It was Tom and Burt Bixby, cowboys, not working now and just hanging around the town since the last trail drive brought them in.

"Sheriff, we found a dead body just now down on the Old River Road. Dead as a stump and still warm."

"Which one are you?" the sheriff said to the man talking and waving his hands in the air.

"I am Tom, Tom Bixby. This is my brother Bert. We were coming up from the river with Clayton Gray. He is still down there with the dead guy."

"Who is dead?" asked Sheriff Martin pulling on his hat.

"That Sam guy, Sam Finn. He is *really* dead. Someone caved in his head."

Martin paused, "I didn't know that there was any other kinda dead." The sheriff got his horse from a shady spot around the corner where he was tied. He slipped the hackamore over his nose, tightened his cinch, mounted up and the three men rode off at a fast trot towards the river. When they got to the site Clayton Cray was sitting on a rock smoking a cigarette. The sheriff didn't like him. He was shifty-eyed and belligerent. He had some sort of hold on the Bixby boys and they followed him around like pet dogs. They laughed too hard at his jokes and seemed to keep at arms length. The sheriff suspected they were rustling unbranded cattle and that is why they were coming back along the River Road this way.

The man on the rock pointed to the side of the road where an arm and a leg were seen sticking out from under the bushes. It was laying like someone had tried to get it off of the road and hide it there. Martin pushed the brush aside and almost gasped as he saw the back of the man's head. The scalp was lifted up and the bone caved in. He noticed that the clothes, mainly the fly of the pants was open and the belt undone on his trousers. His shirt was pulled open, which had pulled off a couple of buttons. The pocket inside the shirt was empty. Martin looked around the area and found the empty billfold ten feet away. He picked it up and brought it back to the body.

"Looks like someone killed and robbed him," he said to himself out loud.

Clayton and the Bixby boys milled around looking for anything but finding nothing but the original blood spot in the middle of the road. Deputy Marion Fitz, known as Buck, pulled up with the buckboard. They loaded the body, covered it with a canvas and headed back to town. The word was already out when they arrived in town. People gathered around muttering to each other and gawked about waiting for a look at the corpse. One of the people that wandered close was Bobby with Dog near his side fanning the air with his huge tail. On his overalls dangled the chain with the watch on the end bouncing loosely in his pocket. Someone said loudly "Hey, that's Sam Finn's chain." The chain was pulled out and the watch came out of his pocket for everyone to see. People started crowding towards Bobby. He became nervous acting, fidgety, and began walking away backwards not liking the close contact that he was not used to. The sheriff stopped him just as he had turned and started to appear like he was going to run away.

"Bobby," said the sheriff quietly. "Where did you get the watch?"

"Mr. Finn gave it to me," he said.

"Mr. Finn gave it to you Bobby? Why was that?"

"He said that I had to take it for the payment for the wood I brought 'em."

"You had to take it?"

"Yes, sir. I wanted two dollars. I can't even tell time. I can't read no watch."

The crowd began to grumble. Clayton Gray the loudest of all. Gray piped up, "The idjet killed him!"

Sheriff Martin looked at the group crowding close. Others around began to grumble and agree.

"Come on, Bobby, come with me. I think you need protection." Big George rapidly led him over and took him into the office closing the door behind him. Bobby stood there scared stiff with his hands at his sides. "What happened Bobby? Did you kill Sam?"

"Oh no! No, no, no, sir."

"You look kinda bad with the watch, Bobby."

"I never wanted no watch."

They paused then with a long silence.

"I have to keep you here."

"You do?"

"Yes, for your own protection, at least."

"What about my mule and my dog?" Bobby began crying like the little boy that he was.

"I will see that they are well taken care of for you. You can even have Dog in here, if you want."

"I didn't do it!" he blubbered.

"I believe you, Bobby. I believe you."

Sheriff George Martin felt worried and uneasy as he locked Bobby in the cell behind his desk. Bobby curled up on the cot with his face to the wall blubbering quietly awhile and then went to sleep with his dog on the floor by his feet.

"What a mess," George said to himself. He stared at the wall awhile then picked up the law books he was studying. He was finished with the correspondence course from Philadelphia. As soon as he got a license, he would be a full-fledged lawyer. He mused to himself, "The whole thing is just words. You just have to know the party of the first part from the party of the second part, the executor from the executrix. Just a bunch of words to confuse common sense." These words he muttered to himself for the hundredth time as he obediently took out his long list of legal words. He was a slow reader at first but was now much faster with the amount of practice over these last two years. The dictionary that he used at first was required less and less in the course of his already two-year-long studies. He was smart and he knew it. He was wise also having seen all kinds of crime and there was not a naïve bone in his body. He knew these things with himself and from them came a confidence which inspired other people.

After reading, studying, scratching words and notes for a couple of hours he put on the glasses that he only needed for distant vision and went over and looked out the window. Marion Fitz, Buck, was walking up the street toward the sheriff's office carrying his ever-present .25/.35 Winchester carbine and wearing the smile that sometimes looked like it was painted on his face. George was glad to see him. His deputy. His trusted friend and mayor of Sweetwater, Arizona, the most ridiculously misnamed place in all of the Arizona territory in the 1880s. The sheriff smiled to himself and almost laughed out loud at the clumsy way the bowlegged cowpoke and former bronco buster climbed the two stairs up to the door.

"All right, what the hell are you laughing at?" demanded Buck. "Never mind, I know and you know what you can do, don't you?" Buck tried to sound grumpy but inside himself he was chuckling too.

"Bobby is sleeping on the cot there with his dog. My God, what am I runnin' here? Anyhow, I will go over to Frances' Café and order up some meals for him. They will bring them over, but you put them inside, you hear? Got a real killer-tough hombre in there." He paused for a moment and looked hard at Buck. "For Christ sake, what bullshit. That guy wouldn't hurt a fly. Besides, something is bothering me."

"What's that?" asked Buck as he laid his rifle against the wall and took a seat.

"Old man Sam's wallet was thrown off into the bushes empty as Bobby's head. Where did the money go? Bobby ain't got but a half dollar and a broken worthless watch to his name." With this the sheriff took his own sawed-off double-barrel shotgun under his arm and meandered out of the door without looking back.

His brow was knitted up and he looked more at his feet than anything else. Unusual for him because he was usually busy scrutinizing the town and streets as he walked. Buck laughed at him. "My legs is right bowed fer sure, but your haid, looks like it is on a swivel and you ain't even got a neck," he said out loud to no one. "You are put together like an eagle bird."

Sheriff George Martin entered Frances' Café and told Frances to bring over food and drink for Bobby if she would be so kind. "Feed him twice a day, say at ten o'clock and then maybe at six." George looked at his pocket watch. "It is three now and I know he hasn't ate all day now. Maybe you could feed him early today? Huh?"

"Yes, I see to it. I give him frijoles, bacon, and biscuits. He comes around sometimes and I give him a sack of biscuits for his job here. I think he gives half of them to his mule and his dog." Frances chuckled to herself and got busy behind the curtain leading to the kitchen. At first she laughed loudly then looked back through the curtain at George with a scowl.

"He didn't kill anyone," she said. "There are bad hombres in town but he is not one of them. Watch out for him, sheriff, there are bad hombres around here." She said no more, left and disappeared again into the kitchen. Sheriff stood for a moment where he was. "Shit," he said and left out onto the street.

He walked faster now, a little irritated by his newly acquired burden. He kicked dust on purpose, raising a cloud as he stomped down the street into the livery stable. Buck used to own it but sold out to the guy who bought the mercantile store. A nice, good businessman and a real asset to Sweetwater. His name was Warren Pullen. He was a Jack Mormon with six good kids and a servantile wife who hardly ever spoke above a whisper and always looked like she was apologizing for something. He had never seen Warren speak to her except to give very polite words that he tried to make sound like requests.

Anyhow, he was likable and George was glad to see him as he eyed Warren's stable establishment.

"Howdy, Warren."

"Well howdy-do, Sheriff. I am glad you came by. Lookin' after your horse?" he asked. "He is more than fine. Come here and look at this."

The sheriff walked over to where Warren was pointing. There was a brand-new saddle there sitting on a sawhorse. It was a beauty. The south Texas stock saddle with a low cantel for swinging off fast and a large wide saddle horn that looked like it could hold any longhorn steer. Saddles are a cowboy's prize possession. Lots of times their only possession. Since Sheriff George Martin was a cowboy and a ranger in his earlier days with hours and days in the saddle on all kinds of caballos in all kinds of conditions, he could respect and admire and appreciate a saddle such as this. His mind went over the makings of a good saddle. The saddletree is hand carved from a well-seasoned piece of wood that was tough, but had spring to it like an old big oak that had grown where it had plenty of water—so the rings weren't too close together and there were few knots and no splits. The spring was important to give with shifting motions of the horse in different gates and positions. Uphill, downhill, over rocks and across water in a walk, a gallop or a dead run. The wood tree, properly carved with the saddle horn one piece not added on, was then covered with rawhide, sewn in place and soaked with salt water. Each layer of leather was cut from prime cattle hide, loosened, softened, and massaged with leather oil until it was just limber enough to conform to the legs, seat, and stirrups. This one had large tapaderos over the stirrups to protect the boot from the cactus, and to prevent a foot from being caught in the stirrup in case of leaving the horse unexpected and not ready. Many men have died from having their foot caught in and then dragged by a crazed horse until they were near pulp. *Tapaderos are a good thing*, he thought. George wondered why anyone who worked every day in the saddle and knew the dangers would do without these. This saddle was shined with beeswax and seemed to glow in the sun. George whistled and touched the leather smooth under his hands.

"Is this for you?" he asked.

"Nope, had it made down in south Texas by a guy who

owed me money. It is for sale. Hell, no one around here has enough money to buy this saddle except Sam Finn and he is dead so he has no use for it. Well, someone will come along," said Warren. He paused, "Someday. Anyhow no one will use it and we can all admire it." He let out a good-natured laugh, turned to leave, waved over his shoulder and laughed again and said, "Your damn horse is spoiled but you can see he is fine. You owe me fifty cents a week, you know."

The sheriff stood with his hands pushed down into his rear pockets and laughed back at him. He thought about the saddle and was glad to have his mind away from his present problems. How much he wondered. *Too much for me, anyhow,* he thought. He waved at the stable hand and went back to his office in a better mood.

Nothing much happened in the next few days. The sheriff learned by telegraph that the federal judge, Judge Sage from Tucson, would be by to hold trial in about a week or ten days. George and Buck took turns staying at the office then looking after Bobby. Bobby himself looked happy enough getting fed twice a day. He sure could eat. He loved bacon, beans and biscuits, and asked Frances for them everyday. Buck and the sheriff learned that the dog liked them too. Once and awhile they would go get his mule and bring it around to the window so Bobby could rub his nose and talk to him and he would think they loved each other. Maybe they did. A man can love a dog, his horse, even a cat, I guess. So why couldn't he love a mule?

One evening on the way to his cabin on the edge of town, sheriff passed by Clayton Gray walking his horse through town toward the bar. The Bixby boys were riding with him at sort of respectful distance. Clayton sat upon a nice enough gray horse that he had never seen before, but the remarkable thing was that he was sporting that beautiful south Texas saddle. The sheriff stopped and eyed him and his horse but mostly the saddle. The three cowboys ignored him completely and rode without speaking. Clayton glanced at him then looked quickly away.

"That troubles me," said the sheriff to himself. The picture in his mind was the empty billfold laying under the bushes where it had been thrown.

It was Buck's turn to spend the night in the jail. So after dinner at Frances', Sheriff Martin went on home, lit a fire in his small stove and put on a pot of water for coffee. There was a shuffle of feet on his plank porch, then a timid scratching knock on his door. He started to say come in, thought better of it and went over and opened the door. A boy stood there not moving. Paco looked frightened, frozen. George looked him over evaluating things rapidly

"Come in and sit down, Paco. What's on your mind?"

Reluctantly Paco came in and sat squirming in a chair.

"Spit it out, boy."

"It were me, sheriff, that killed Finn. I killed him not Bobby."

There was silence in the room as a puzzled expression appeared on the sheriff's face. "You killed him?"

"Yes."

"How?"

"With his ax. I hit him with his ax."

"Why? "

"He was on top of my sister trying to er . . . er . . . get her. He slapped her in the face and she was crying. He was on top of her pulling up her dress, so I hit him with the ax to make him stop and leave her alone. He was a bad man and I am not sorry I hit him. I didn't mean to kill him though."

The sheriff sat down across the table with a look of disgust on his face. "That dirty old son of a bitch. Rose was just a little girl. You really whacked him, Paco?"

"I hit him as hard as I could."

"Tell me, what in hell's name went on that day?"

The boy looked George Martin square in the eye with a matter of fact look on his face, only tinged by anger and said, "I was supposed to be cuttin' up wood for Sam Finn. All he had to use was an ax with a broken handle. It were cracked and it weren't any good. It was dull too. He made me try to fix it but I knew that it weren't any good. Rosa was on the way to the river. I saw the way that he looked at her. He had the look of the devil himself. He didn't think that I would notice but I saw him sneak down the River Road following where she went. I worried fer her. I thought I had an excuse. The axe handle cracked again so I decided to go down to the river and git a dried up piece of mesquite to make another. But, really, I wanted to be sure that Rosa was all right, so I followed Finn."

"It was a good thing that you did. Go on."

"Well, I heard noises. Rosa was cryin' like I said. Sam Finn was on top of her gruntin' and slobberin' and sweatin' like a pig. I couldn't let him. I wouldn't let him . . . er . . . git her like that, the fat, bastard, gringo son of a bitch. I just ran up and whacked him. I am not sorry, but I didn't mean to kill him"

"Ya, you did that!"

"Well, I told Rosa to go home and I tried to roll him off the road under the bushes but he was too big. Rosa ran home. I heard horses comin' so I took the axe and ran off to the bushes outta there. I didn't know what else to do. I were scared. Rosa didn't want me to tell anyone what happened to her but when I found out that Bobby was arrested, I knew I had to tell what I did. I couldn't let Bobby . . . er . . . "

George looked hard across the table at Paco who sat perfectly still with his hands fidgety on the table but otherwise in total control.

"What about the money, boy?"

Paco looked confused.

"The dinero, all the money he had in his billfold. What did you do with that?"

Paco shook his head vigorously. "No, no, I don't know nothin' bout no money."

"You didn't take his billfold out of his shirt?"

Paco looked worried at the accusation. He slipped into native Spanish for a moment even though his English was about perfect. "No, Senior Sir, I took nada. I know nothin' 'bout any money." His eyes were wide and he looked apprehensive.

George stood up and walked over to his stove and began building his fire again. He thought of Gray sitting on a rock smoking his cigarette when the Bixby boys brought him up there. "Don't worry muchacho. I believe you."

"Will I have to go to jail?" Paco said shuffling his feet and looking at his restless hands.

"Hell no, you won't have to go to jail." George busied himself pouring water and coffee into the pot. He put the pot on the stove, on the hottest part just in front of the stovepipe. "You will have to tell it to a judge, but don't worry just tell him the truth like you did me. I would leave off the 'hard as I could part' though, if I was you," he chuckled.

The room was silent again as the two looked at each other without speaking The silence was broken by the sound of a horse galloping up to the porch and Buck yelling for the sheriff. George raced to the door as Buck rained in.

"They broke Bobby outta jail. They're fixin' to lynch him. They knocked me in the head when I wasn't looking. They shot his dog and drug him outta the cell while I was layin' on the floor. I wasn't out cold but I just couldn't move to stop them or even get up."

"My God! Who was it?"

"Gray and them two Bixby boys."

"That figures," George said. He grabbed his double-barrel shot-gun, opened it to be sure that it was filled with buck-shot, then climbed up behind Buck on his big round horse. "They will take him to that Palo Verde tree behind the saloon. Let's go!" he yelled.

Buck touched his spurs to the over-burdened horse, but it made no protest and galloped at full speed back to town. When they arrived at the tree, a small crowd of men had gathered around grumbling and looking over their shoulders. They all looked guilty of something, like they didn't like what was happening. They all wanted to stop but no one moved to do so. They had Bobby with his hands tied behind him sitting on his own mule. Gray was pulling on the mule's head lead rope, cussing up a storm and Burt Bixby was pushing on his tail as hard as he could. The mule would not budge. "Damn it, Burt, get behind him and quirt the hell outta him." Burt did as he was told with his usual dull look on his ugly face. The mule would not move. The second time that Burt hit him with the quirt both feet flew back lightening quick hitting Burt square in the middle and sending him sprawling to the ground. The people there laughed out loud. Clayton Gray with a red face and bulging eyes yelled something about what an idiot and proclaiming that he was going to kill the mule.

"I'll get you off there. I will jerk you off," he said to Bobby.

The rope was draped over a branch of the tree and tied to the trunk near the ground. The noose was around Bobby's neck. When Clayton grabbed Bobby and yanked him sideways off the mule, the sheriff's shotgun roared. Both barrels shattered the branch to pieces blowing the rope apart. Bobby fell harmlessly to the ground choking on the noose around his neck until someone jumped up from the crowd, ran forward with a sharp knife and divided the rope releasing him from the hateful grip. Bobby laid on the ground for a moment and then the man cut the ropes from his wrists. Bobby, still without saying anything, lay on the ground and rubbed his neck.

The sheriff stepped forward, unarmed, as his shotgun was now empty and he had not grabbed his pistol when he left his cabin. Buck was beside him, however, with his 25-35 Carbine cocked—leveled and ready.

"You, Gray, you Bixby boys, you are all under arrest for attempted murder. Now undo your gun belts and drop them to the grounds right now, pronto, do you understand?" They just stood there. Clay and Tom that is. Burt still lay on the ground moaning and retching. No one was helping him.

"You can't do . . . " That's all that Clayton Gray got out of his twisted mouth before Buck put a round right between his feet.

"Do as he says now, you assholes!" yelled Buck. "The next one goes right into your balls." The two dropped their guns with sullen anger on their faces.

"Now get that puking coyote up out of the dirt, undo his gun belt and let's go to jail, boys, peaceful like. All three of you, you are all under arrest for attempted murder."

Buck waved his gun barrel as further instruction and looked eager to pull steel if he had too. The three men were pushed into the cell where the dead dog lay stretched and bleeding on the floor. Buck gave Tom an extra hard push that sent him stumbling over the dog. "Hey get this thing outta here!" he yelled.

"You don't give the orders here, shithead," said Buck, "besides you might want to use him for a pillow since one of you has to sleep on the floor."

It was four long hot days before Buck and the sheriff could no longer stand the smell of the three men living so closely—let alone with the dead dog there too. They were told to carry the dog out respectfully and bury him out back. Each was shackled at the ankles, fixed with horse hobbles made of chain and secured with a padlock. They lurched their way along carrying the unwrapped dog like a bundle in their arms. The dog was heavy. They had to take turns carrying him, sweating and cursing as they went. The small shovel they were given was dull and rusted and very short handled.

"Get digging, boys," said Buck.

Tom Bixby protested, "This ground is hard. We need a pick and a decent shovel. This will take all day. It's hot as an oven out here."

"You don't get no pick. You got nowhere to go anyway, do you? Now get at it. I want it four-feet deep. You can have all the water you want as long as you keep on working."

Bobby had appeared from behind the building and stood staring at them all day while they dug the grave of his dog. "I put him in," he said when they were done. He lowered the dog down gently with little-boy heartbreak on his face. "Now you can cover him nice!" he ordered as he walked away without looking back.

2

Judge Charles Sage was due to come up from Tucson. A federal territory judge, he went on a circuit to where he was needed. He was five days away when Clayton Gray began to shout that they wanted an attorney. It was their right and they were entitled. Since there was only one lawyer around there, there wasn't any choice. Harley Fletcher was new to Sweetwater, a young man in his thirties who was a westerner in the mining business before he had gone back to New York to law school years before. He was generally a good man and honest but he didn't have much business yet he augmented his income a few since by being a carpenter in town. He agreed without reluctance and met privately with the prisoners, while Buck or the sheriff stood guard outside the door.

"My God, they stink! I demand that you treat these men humanely!" he proclaimed as he left the jail.

"All right," said Sheriff George. "The trial is in two days. Tomorrow we will take him down to the river so that they can take a bath and wash their clothes, how's that?"

"That would be just fine," said Lawyer Fletcher with an unexpected good-natured grin.

"That man will never make no lawyer," said Buck as Fletcher walked away, "Too nice a fella."

Judge Charles Sage came to Sweetwater when the church was commandeered to be used as the courtroom. It was a good place and, as a matter of fact, it was the only place that held enough people except maybe the saloon which is no place for a trial.

Judge Sage was appointed federal territory judge who was well known to be well educated in the east. Most thought that he was way too lenient, others thought he was just too damn kind. Of course he drank too much but never when his court was in session—just afterwards and before. He sat at a desk which had been hauled in for him and put in the center in front of the pulpit. He rapped with a little hammer and said kind of pompous-like, "Court in and for the territory of Arizona is now in session. Everybody be quiet. Don't speak unless you are spoken to and mind your manners. All right, sheriff, let's begin."

The sheriff stepped forward. "Judge Sage, this is Paco Rivas. He came to me voluntarily and told me about the incident that lead to the death of Sam Finn. He confessed that Finn died at his hands. I would like him to tell it to you like he told it to me."

"Go on then," said the judge.

George Martin told Paco to come up before Judge Sage. He did so slowly but directly and deliberately. He stood there with his hat in his hand going from one foot to the other nervously on weak knees. "Give him a chair before he falls down," said the judge. The sheriff brought a straight-back chair over and slid it in place before the desk. "You swear by God to tell the truth," the judge directed more than asked.

"Yes," was the timid answer.

"Speak up so I can hear you. Sit down." Paco sat down awkwardly and looked all around. He saw his mother and father with Rosa sitting between them sitting in the back row. Rosa's eyes were looking down at her hands folded on her lap, not moving. Seeing her gave him courage. He was not ashamed of what he did and he would do it again if he had to.

"Tell the judge what happened the day that Sam Finn was killed, Paco. Tell him it just like you told me," said the sheriff, who gave him a quick pat on the back and stepped away.

Paco spoke English very well with hardly a hint of an accent. He spoke loud enough and directly to the judge. His eyes never left the judge's face and neither of them looked away. Paco told it just as he had done before to the sheriff. All of it except he left out the part, "I hit him as hard as I could," and just said, "I hit him to make him stop." It was well done and Paco looked impressive, confident and completely honest. Judge Sage stirred in his chair, looked up at George Martin and around the room.

"This is a case of justifiable homicide if I ever heard one. I dismiss the case completely and any charges against you are hereby and forever dropped."

Sheriff Martin took Paco by the shoulder nudging him out of the chair and pointing him towards the family. "Adios muchacho. You done good," he said quietly.

Paco walked out of the church, without looking about, with his mother, brother and sister behind him. Someone started cheering a little and clapping quietly and soon everyone except the judge had joined in. The judge allowed it without comment then raised his hand to make it stop. The Rivas folks were in full smile as they left.

"All right, Sheriff, let's get on with it. You have three men here charged with" he picked up and read from a paper, "attempted murder, interfering and attacking an officer of the law, discharging a firearm inside of a building and killing a dog. Ain't no law against killing a dog, but proceed. You are the prosecutor. I see that they have a lawyer."

"Good morning, your Honor. I am Harley Fletcher, a licensed lawyer and represent these accused." He stood and laid his brand-new briefcase on a small table in front of him. He was fine looking, with a new waistcoat and a new licked down smooth haircut as well.

"Huh," was all the judge said, while looking him over then motioned for him to sit down. He then looked at the chair and simply nodded toward him. Sheriff George Martin began with a look of disdain at the Bixby boys and Clayton Gray. They sat looking nowhere in particular, but obviously confident in their new lawyer.

"Your Honor, before Paco Rivas came and confessed to me I had another suspect locked up in the jail." He looked about locating Bobby sitting in an aisle seat in the second row right behind Warren, who was acting as the official record keeper.

"This was Bobby . . . er . . . Bobby, what is your last name?"

"I ain't got one, far as I know."

Sheriff paused for a moment looking at the uncomfortable man. "Smith, could it be Smith?"

"Yes, sir, it could be Smith."

The people tittered but only a moment, as the judge rapped lightly on his desk and looked stern.

"Good, good," said the sheriff, "I had Bobby Smith locked up while we began the investigation. There was the matter of the dead man's watch being in his possession, which has since been cleared up. While in legal custody of my jail, these three gallutes here took it upon themselves to have a lynching. Lynching of a man who has been shown to be perfectly innocent. They came into the jail, accosted and attacked Deputy Marion Fitz there." He pointed to Buck sitting next to the recorder. "Knocked him on the head and took Mr. Smith from the jail cell, shot his dog in the process. Then they drug him out, put him on his own mule, and took him off to the big Palo Verde tree behind town where they commenced to put a noose around his neck, and attempted to kill him by hanging. The mule would not even budge. If it had, it would have been too late. The mule kicked what's his name,

Bixby over there, right in the belly." Everyone in the courtroom laughed out loud and even the judge chuckled at the vision of the absurd scene before he tapped again for silence. "Clayton Cray then jerked him off sideways. I fired my shotgun into the branch, breaking the rope just in time where Bobby Smith would have had a broken neck or strangled to death." There was a long pause as the sheriff-prosecutor walked over to the three, pointed at each one and said, loudly with authority, "I then arrested them for attempted murder, assaulting a peace officer in the execution of his work, discharging a firearm inside of a building, illegal by city ordinance, your Honor, and killing another man's possession, his dog."

"Do you want to examine these suspects on the stand now, Sheriff?" asked the judge as if helping him with the usual procedure of the trial.

"Your Honor, I wish to hold my examination until after their attorney Mr. Harley Fletcher here has his say, if you have no objection," he added, "And he has none either," George added.

"I have no objection," said Fletcher still sitting.

"Me neither, then," said the judge, "proceed, Mr. Fletcher.

Harley Fletcher stood up dramatically and faced the judge with quiet concern on his face and paused for effect.

"Mr. Fletcher, proceed then," the judge said again.

The lawyer stood, looking wrinkle-browed and serious and concerned all at the same time, and began.

"Your Honor, we certainly do not deny the facts as stated by Mr. Sheriff Prosecutor here. They are unfortunately the facts. An innocent man was almost lynched by total error but he wasn't. They took the law into their own hands. Lynchings have gone on all over the west for a hundred years. I am not saying that it is right, but it occurs."

He paused and walked around his table again with his hands grasped behind him and his head down as if contemplating a serious matter. "Can we call it murder or attempted murder? Many times in the course of Arizona history, citizens have found it necessary and advisable to administer quick and permanent justice like a duty to avoid permanent injustice. Like a duty to avoid delays and loopholes in the law that often allowed unscrupulous villains to go free or escape before our ragged infantile system could accomplish a thing. People, my clients, felt only that they were doing their duty as they had by history been led to believe their duty was. These poor cow folks didn't know any better from their own experiences or by history in this territory or in Texas where they came from either." He shook his head, "No."

"A shame, just a shame to learn that that behavior was not acceptable anymore. They were merely following what they thought was right and they were being good citizens. After all, the record in Arizona will support this belief, will it not?" Everyone sort of shook their heads and muttered agreement. "After all, how did they know he was innocent when the case seemed so solid against him. He was in possession of the man's watch for heaven's sake and everyone knew it." He paced around some more looking dramatic with a wrinkled-up look of concern on his face. "This is difficult for me to say, I wish to be fair to Bobby Smith." He paused a moment then went over and put his hand on Bobby's shoulder. Bobby didn't look up at him. He hadn't looked up once since he came in the church court and he didn't look up now. Mr. Fletcher patted him lightly then turned to face the judge. "Bobby Smith is not right in the head, your Honor. He is not very intelligent and we all know it." He looked all around the room for approval. "People so afflicted are given to unpredictable and often aggressive, angry, heinous behavior. What were these poor, uneducated cowboys to surmise?"

Heinous and surmise—two words that few people in the room did not know but caught the meaning of immediately. It added to the lawyer's convincing manner. He waiting a long time then strode back to his desk. "Your Honor, I know you know and understand the legality and the importance of legal precedence in the law of our land. Perhaps the prosecutor here doesn't. Briefly, once a precedent has been set by a legal decision, it is to be customarily and legally honored until and if the law has been changed. I have here the records of two lynching matters in Arizona. One from Tucson in 1876 and one from Oxbow in 1880 for your perusal, Judge." He sauntered over and handed the two court records to the judge with exaggerated humility. "With utmost respect, Judge Sage," he said earnestly, "perhaps Mr. Martin would like to see them also." George was just sitting quietly in the front row.

"No, thank you, Councilor. I have reviewed them and I know quite well what is in them cases," Martin said without looking up. Mr. Fletcher looked surprised to say the least, stunned would be closer.

"Oh yes," he finally managed to say, "I understand you are studying law." George said nothing.

"We have to see what has been done before in the legal system. In Tucson in 1876, three people were taken out by a lynch mob from jail, I might add, and summarily hanged for their crimes. There crimes had not even been proven yet and as it turned out, one, the woman, was later discovered to be innocent. The instigators of the lynching were tried and convicted of disorderly and destructive conduct and fined twenty-five dollars each and released. A legal precedent had been set. The judge felt that they had thought simply that they were doing their legal duty in a corrupt and inefficient legal system. Many people had been known and still are to this day to bribe their way out of every single charge." He punctuated every single charge by thumping his fist into his hand. "Let us consider the Oxbow," he said. "A shame, a miserable shame. Three innocent men were lynched for rustling cattle. A crime that they were innocent of, mind you. A shame, a shame," he said again. "What was the finding of this case? Germaine it is by the case in hand. These men thought that they were doing their duty as citizens and their only honest intention was to see that justice was done and done quickly to protect people and property," he added. "You know that they too were simply fined twenty-five dollars? No further action was taken against them." He paused again looking squarely at the judge who did not flinch or react in any visible way.

"Precedent," said Mr. Fletcher, "legal and under the knowledge of the citizens justifiable." He walked over to the three men who were not very successfully trying to hide smiles and Clayton Gray himself smirked. He turned back to the judge and walked over to him quickly like he had been called. "So you see, these cowboys are honest, uninformed folks who by the knowledge of how things were done erroneously and regretfully took the law into their own hands. Regretful? Yes. Wrong? Yes. But murder or attempted murder? I think not. Their only motive was to speed up and ensure the wheels of justice as they had been led to believe for so many years was necessary in our frontier. Murder or attempted murder? Not hardly. Murder implies a motive. The only motive here in the cases that I quoted was to perpetuate and to ensure rapid punishment to those who spit in the face of decent law-abiding people."

Fletcher was impressive. He was waiting until all that he had said had fully sunk in. "I ask that these men with no prior history of violence for law breaking be fined twenty-five dollars and released to continue to contemplate with their true regret and remorse, which will never leave them for their deeds for this regrettable action. Thank you for your attention, and the attention of the citizens in this room."

Without saying a word, Judge Sage looked over at the sheriff-prosecutor. George Martin stood. "As I requested, your Honor, I would now want to examine the accused to present my factual case further. I understand that Mr. Fletcher had not questioned the facts as presented thus far. He will have the opportunity to question new ones further and cross-examine my witnesses. Could we have recess until after lunch so I can gather my witnesses and evidence?"

The judge stirred in his seat, "Yes, that is a right smart idea. Adjourned until one o'clock."

What in the hell, thought Mr. Fletcher. *What evidence for God's sake? What witnesses?*. The thoughts stirred around in his head. He shook his head and prepared to leave for lunch.

After the break they all paraded in and sat exactly where they were before, but there were more people there and some had to be content, just looking in the windows.

The sheriff began, "Judge, may I have banker Tubbs up here so I can question him?"

"You may," answered the judge.

"I object!" shouted Attorney Fletcher,

"On what grounds?" asked the judge.

"What does a banker have to do with this case?"

"I don't know, but we aim to find out, now don't we? Overruled," he added.

"Now sit down."

"Mr. Tubbs, as the banker here in Sweetwater did you receive a package of brand new bills from San Francisco by stagecoach the day before Sam Finn was killed?"

'Objection!" arose Mr. Fletcher again. "The witness has not been duly sworn in."

Judge Sage looked a little annoyed. "We can play these sort of games if you want to. You are correct he hasn't been sworn in so we will swear him in. Do you hereby swear to tell the truth and nothing but the truth, so help you God?"

"I do," said Mr. Tubbs.

"Proceed then and answer the question."

"Yes, I do," he repeated, "I did receive the new bills."

"Were you given a list of the serial numbers of these bills?" inquired the sheriff.

"Yes, I was."

"And did you give a sizable sum to Mr. Finn the morning of his death?"

"I did."

"And did you keep a record of the serial numbers you gave him?"

"I did. I gave out no other money of any kind that day."

"May we have a list of those serial numbers?"

"Certainly," the banker said and handed a paper to the sheriff who glanced at it and handed it to the judge.

"Thank you, Mr. Tubbs. You are excused unless Mr. Fletcher has any questions."

"No questions," Mr. Fletcher said.

"Now, Mr. Warren Pullen will you come here and be sworn?"

Mr. Pullen raised his hand, said his "I do," and sat down.

"You own the Mercantile Store here, we all know. Not a question but we all know," he added quickly. The sheriff anticipated the objection but none was made. "You have . . . had the beautiful Texas stock saddle for sale, did you not?"

"I did, yes."

"What happened to that saddle?"

"It was bought by Clay Gray, paid in cash. Yes, brand new bills they were."

"Do you have that cash still in your possession?"

"Yes, I do."

"Will you please tell Judge Sage why and how you happen to have it?"

"You came to my office last week and asked me about the sale of the saddle. You asked to see the money."

"The exact money?"

"Yes, the exact same money that Gray gave me."

"What did you do with it?"

"Well, after we looked at it, you asked me to put it into an envelope, glue it shut. You glued some horsehairs across the seal and signed your name over the horse hairs with an ink pen. You then told me to keep the envelope in my possession at all times."

"You did that?"

"Yes, never left my possession. I even slept with it"

"Good. Now will you show us the envelope." He was already holding it in his hands. "Has my signature been in any way changed? Are the horsehairs still glued there, undisturbed?"

"Yes, they are and, no, your signature across the horsehairs ain't been disturbed at all."

"Your Honor, I did all these things to establish the line of possession of this important evidence. That is the reason for all this hooplah." The sheriff took the envelope from Mr. Pullen and showed it to the judge. He looked it over, nodded his head and handed it back. The sheriff did not take it, but held up his hand to stop him.

"Your Honor, would you be so kind to open the envelope and compare the serial numbers with the list Mr. Tubbs gave you?" The judge did as he was asked, quickly comparing the serial numbers.

"For the record," he said "these are the same numbers, all right. Do you have any questions, Mr. Fletcher?" The lawyer just shook his head no without answering. The sheriff looked at Mr. Warren Pullen, thanked him and excused him. He got up and left with a serious smile on his face. The judge then looked at Clayton Gray. "Gray sit down up here!" Gray did not move. "Now!" said the judge. Clayton Gray came forward slowly, looking seriously worried, and then sat down. "Where did you get the cash, Clayton?" the sheriff demanded. Clayton did not answer. He stared at his attorney for help but none was coming. "You had to have taken it from Finn, that is obvious. Was he dead or alive when you took it?"

"He was already dead!" Clayton exclaimed loudly, "He was dead as a stump already."

"We didn't know nothin' bout no money!" Burt and Tom Bixby said almost together. "We didn't know nothin' 'bout it! We had nothin' to do with robbin' nobody."

"You boys shut up and don't speak again until you are asked a question! You hear me?" said the judge.

"Your Honor, Judge Sage, the council for the defense said that these boys acted only as citizens after justice and right. Clayton, you tried to lynch Bobby Smith to hide your own theft hoping the matter would end there. That is so, isn't it? You were looking out for your own ass and that's all, right? Am I right?" he asked again.

"Objection!" Lawyer Fletcher half-heartedly crowed. "Calls for speculation and supposition on the prosecutor's part."

Judge Sage glared at him, "sounds like a pretty damn good supposition to me and not much speculation. Overruled. You answer the question." Clayton Gray sat silently with his lips twitching, clenching and unclenching his hands.

"It is apparent that you ain't going to answer," addressed the sheriff. "It is apparent that you didn't act for any reason other than to smoke screen and hide your miserable theft." He looked down at his desktop for a few seconds before continuing in a slow, deliberate and dignified manner.

Judge Sage shouted and pounded his table. "Sheriff, put the cuffs on him. I find him guilty of attempted murder and sentence him to fifteen years at hard labor in the Yuma Prison!"

The sheriff took a step towards Buck to get the handcuffs from him. Quick as a cat, Clayton leaped to his feet and grabbed the pistol from Sheriff Martin's holster.

"No one is sending me to prison for robbing a dead man and trying to hang a worthless Indian nigger idjet. No one move, no one gets shot!" He backed up a few short steps then turned to run up the aisle. Bobby Smith sitting in the aisle seat stuck out his foot and tripped the off-balanced fleeing man. He went sprawling across the floor with a gun in front of him. Tom Bixby standing there stomped down on Clayton's gun hand with his heel. The pistol came loose from his grip and then his brother Burt kicked it rattling across the floor back to the sheriff. George grabbed it up and leveled it at the man, now sobbing there on the floor.

"We didn't know nothin' bout no damn money," said Burt again quietly. Lawyer Fletcher had not moved through all of this. He came slowly to this feet, took a billfold out of his coat pocket and layed several crisp bills on his table.

"I don't think I can keep these," he said with a sigh. Then he stepped over the blubbering Clayton Gray as the sheriff was putting the handcuffs on him behind his back. He paused looking down into Sheriff Martin's face. "You know what, I knew I had lost this case when you said you already knew what was in those case histories from Tucson and Oxbow. You are a better lawyer than me." With that he left without ever looking back.

Epilogue

The judge determined that the Bixby boys didn't know anything about the stolen money, and were just plain stupid and led into their actions by Clayton Smith. He gave them until sundown to get out of town and a week to get out of Arizona Territory—never to return there. It helped their cause when they helped disarm their leader. He found that there was also no sense in fining them because they never had any money anyhow. Clayton Gray was taken in handcuffs and a ball and chain to Yuma Prison to serve his fifteen years at hard labor. They let him out in five years.

Sam Finn's money, after all his holdings were sold at auction, was split 50/50 with Bobby and Rosa. Bobby left town and was never seen or heard from again. It was said that Rosa and her family moved to New Mexico. No one knew what happened to them or their money either.

Warren Pullen got his saddle back.

A while later George Martin became a licensed attorney on Judge Sage's recommendation and moved to Phoenix to set up practice—and to find someone special.

As for me, Marion Fritz, I just stayed on in Sweetwater and thus ends the story Sweetwater, Arizona, about 1889.

Part III

Race, Shot and Swallow

1

I was running the Mercantile Store in Sweetwater when a guy named Charlie Kluntz first started coming into town to trade. He would come on Friday morning. Sitting on a buckboard beside him was his homely, bucktooth scrawny kid, Ronnie. Always thought it fit him, Scrawny Ronnie. I never thought Sweetwater was an unfriendly place, but no one was very nice to him. People just grunted at his friendly waves, hellos and smiles. No doubt he was an odd duck in more than a few ways. Let me describe him.

He was close to six feet, I think. Wiry, but not skinny. He wore an old-fashioned floppy hat, like sod-busters wear. No cowboy would be caught dead in one like that. His clothes always looked clean and in good shape. I mean, no patches or rips but they were just odd for around here.

None of this is unusual, I know. I have to tell you about his problems. He could not stop his head from bobbing back and forth, from front to back, a nice rhythmic rate that never let up but grew faster when he got animated.

People stared. He never seemed to notice. Old Andy said that he looked like a chicken. All he needed was a tin beak and he could be down there scratching shit. My God, when he walked, even his head went a little from side to side too. Then, darned if he didn't resemble a pigeon.

Like I say, people from Sweetwater ain't mean or snobbish but everyone just sort of, well, would rather not be around him, you could say. Folks were afraid they would catch something, I think. As for me, though, I was curious as hell and he paid his bill on the spot with gold or silver.

"Where are you from, Mr. Kluntz?"

"Name's Charlie, Mr. Fitz. Mr. Kluntz was my pappy, my grandpappy. I am from Kentucky and glad to be out of there. Poor soil and mosquitoes the size of buzzards. Kind of hot here in the summers, ain't it? Let me tell you," his voice creaked, rattled and stalled like a rusty door. All in the rhythm of his bobbing head.

"Well now, my name is Buck, not Mr. Fitz," I said. "What you aiming to do here anyways?"

"I am going to be into cattle mostly. I got a nice whole section of land and I am going to get more, gradual, as my herd gets bigger. I got shorthorn Hereford cattle from England. No more damn longhorns

I'd never heard of them at that time. Turns out, they beat hell out of scrawny longhorns."

This guy always had a smile and twinkle in his eyes. It was hard to tell when he was pullin' your leg.

"Also, I am going to raise up angora goats, sheep and rabbits."

"Rabbits? You are going to raise up rabbits?" He looked good-naturedly at me and poked me playfully.

"I don't seem to have much choice. My garden is full of them. They better not get my corn. I need it for my squeezens!"

"You need a couple of dogs."

"I have some pups coming from Kentucky soon. Good Kentucky hounds." (That's another story.)

I asked him if there was a Mrs. Kluntz, looking over at scrawny Ronnie.

"Nope," he said. "Never was, ain't now." I looked at Ronnie with the question on my face. "Oh, him. I just hatched him on a rock."

Looks like it, I said to myself.

Well, he came in from time to time to trade. People just ignored him with sideways glances. Actually, they avoided him despite his grins, waves and howdy-dos.

One time, I just asked him, "If'n you don't mind me askin', Charlie. What? Uh . . . "

"Oh, you mean this," he said pointing to his bobbing head. "Trembly. Milk fever caused it. Kilt a lot of folks but just left me with this. A man puts up with what he has to. I always was of the opinion that it is better than being dead. You know what shaky disease is?"

I just shook my head no.

"Well then, cows eat a kind of plant we called snakeroot. The meadows are filled with it. Poison gets in their flesh and in their milk. Then people get it. Causes people to shake like jelly, then they usually die. If they don't they is left like this sometimes.

"Abe Lincoln's mother died of Trembly," he added.

After that I made an effort to tell folks what it was—that it was nothing catching or anything—but only a few listened.

2

Once a year after the full round-up when the cattle are pastured up for the winter and the ranch hands have time on their hands, we have a horse race and a rifle shoot contest and a Saturday night jamboree dance in a big barn. I put the sign up and sort of run things from the store.

Horse Race Rules
Anyone can enter for $5.00.
Winner takes all.
All bets are on the side between folks or through me.
No odds are given. Bets will be matched equal.
Non-winner's bets left over go to the barn dance fund.
All bets must be in by 12:00 noon, October 15.
The race commences at 12:30 P.M. the same day.
Riders have to register the horse's name, rider and owner.
No changes allowed.
Anyone can enter the rifle-shooting contest for $5.00.
Winner takes all.

Charlie came to town one early afternoon to buy a rain barrel. I just happened to have a couple ten gallons left by an immigrant train that went through a few years back. They were made of solid oak and since they had been kept in the back, they were in good shape. They even had bunghole plugs made of cork.

"How much?" Charlie asked with his eyes sparkling. "This is indeed a blessing."

"What are you going to do with these? It don't rain around here. You can just have them to get 'em out of here. No good to me."

"Obliged," cackled Charlie, pushing 50 cents into my shirt pocket. "I pay my way. Squeezins—corn squeezins. Sour mash Kentucky sippin' whiskey—you will see," he said going out the door with a barrel under each arm.

He deposited them in the back of his buckboard, then stopped to read the sign before coming back in.

"I want to enter," he announced with a flare.

"What?" I asked.

"Why, the horse race and the rifle shoot!"

"You do?"

"Yep, I do."

I walked over to the door and looked out at the horse standing there at his wagon. He did look like a big strong horse, but no runner.

"What is that horse's name?" I asked casually, trying not to grin too much. Charlie's eyes darted over to where I was studying his animal.

"That horse is named William. Ain't he a beaut?"

"Yeh, he is a beaut all right."

"Let's sign me up," Charlie said, walking over to where the book lay on the counter.

"Do you want me to put it in there fer you?" I asked.

"Hell no. I can write better than you."

He picked up the pencil as I looked over his shoulder.

Horse's Name:	Bill
Owner:	Charles Kluntz
Rider:	Ronnie
Entrance Fee:	$5.00

I marked PAID. Charlie reached down in his pockets and

brought up a $20 gold piece. "I want to bet ten dollars with you."

I couldn't help but hesitate.

"Are you sure, Charlie?"

"I am a growed-up man. The other five dollars is for the rifle shoot"

"All right, pardner. Doins are less than a month away. Don't be late—twelve noon.

"I am never late for racin', shootin' or eat'n, he said with a new cackle.

When the day came for the race, I began to wonder if he would show up. There were nine riders in the horse race and as many in the rifle shoot. Right at noon, here he comes in his buckboard with old William pulling, Scrawny Ronnie driving, and what do you think was tied on the dancing rope behind the buckboard. A thin, long-legged, shiny, black horse as slick and beautiful an animal that ever existed. He was a stallion and he was beautiful.

I ran right up to him 'cause I was afraid of trouble.

"You can't enter that there horse. Read the sign. Entrance closed at noon." Charlie stepped down and looked at me like he was puzzled by my statement. "But Captain," he said like he was surprised by it all, "I entered him almost a month ago."

People gathered around as we went in and looked at the book. I noticed right off. It said the horse's name was "Bill."

"The black, that's Bill. You didn't think I meant old William there pulling the buckboard did you? That would be right stupid of me, now wouldn't it?"

Nobody said nothing. I thought we were going to do him out of his money. I knew right then we were about to be done out of ours. Serves us right.

3

The course started out in the center of town, curved around the outskirts to the south, and came around full circle ending up where it started. It was a good two miles which is a long race for a cow pony and involves some knowledgeable pacing and good riding. The boys went bareback to save the weight.

Kluntz brought out a small English saddle that caught everyone's eye.

"He has done this before," I heard someone whisper.

Nine beautiful horses stood prancing around the starting line. The black was a foot taller than any other one. Maybe seventeen hands.

"Ready—Set—Bang," went the starting gun and they were off, fast but not all out. The kid could ride that damn postage stamp. He kept his mount tight in the middle of the pack all the way around the first turn starting back.

"He is holding that horse back," someone said matter of fact.

Yep—he *was* all right. When they were right across from me, I saw him let the reins go loose and tap him with his heels. Damn, he took off like he had been standing still and the rest of the ponies were running backwards!

Blackhorse and rider were way out front when he appeared at the final turn leading back into town. I mean way out in front. They, Ronnie and Black Bill, were pounding down until they were about ten feet from the finish line—then, damned if he didn't pull the critter up and sort of danced him across the finish line. That arrogant, snotty-nosed scrawny man was grinning so wide I thought his buckteeth were going to bite his lips off. No one cheered. No one smiled, let alone laughed. Lots of folks grumbled, Charlie? He looked kind of confused. He laughed out loud at first until he met icy stares and grumbles. Like I said, he looked right confused that everyone else did not share his mirth and humor. He looked hurt for Christ's sake.

He had won it all—the entrance fees and half the bets plus $20. His bet and mine. Obviously he was the only one who bet for him.

There were lots of cold stares, grumbling and quiet assessing as I gave him the money. Damn near ugly tension in the air if you know what I mean.

We had a nice picnic lunch. Charlie and Ronnie stayed off on their own, eating out of their own sack and not getting any of the good grub laid out in the store. They looked pitiful, damn it—confused and like they had hurt feelings again.

After lunch we set up for the rifle-shooting contest. There were six men including Kluntz. Shooting had to be offhand, no rests, no new-fangled telescope sights either. First, big one-gallon-sized jugs were laid out 150 yards out. For the fun of it, they were filled with water so we could watch them explode when they were hit. They stepped up one by one. Two guys missed coming away saying the sun got in their eyes or their sights were off. The last to shoot was Charlie Kluntz.

He stepped to the line, walking like a pigeon smiling all the while. Out of a sack he brings a rifle that was four-feet long, at least. It was a beautiful thing with a shiny black walnut stock and shiny blue steel barrel, an ivory bead on the one end and a buckhorn open sight on the breach. But you know what? The damn thing was a mussel loader! Yep—an old-fashioned mussel loader. At least it had a compression cap.

Without being asked, Charlie addressed the crowd like he was giving a lecture.

"This here is a Kentucky long rifle, finest one ever made. Truly, they were made by German gunsmiths in Philadelphia, but us Kentuckians known how to use 'em."

He took out the ramrod from under the barrel and commenced to load. Paper, powder and the slug were tapped home. He put the compression cap on the nipple and toed the line. He brought the heavy rifle up to his shoulder, his bobbing head came forward, stopped for about a second as he squinted down the barrel, then boom. I mean BOOM. The jug, of course, exploded, but the air was filled with a blue cloud of smoke. Charlie was rocked back and almost fell. Odd, no one laughed.

"Powder's old. Too strong—used too much," he explained to nobody listening.

Next round, the jugs were half the size. Two more guys missed. Charlie didn't miss. That left just the two of them. Thomas Pelton was an old-timer. Used to be a buffalo hunter. It was said he could shoot the wings off of a bumblebee. He was a loudmouth braggart in a way, but he was pleasant, comical and everyone liked him and so all were rooting for him. Two plain beer bottles put up as targets at 150 yards, that is small. First Thomas took aim, took his time and squeezed off. The bottle popped and people cheered, Thomas grinned widely. Then Charlie Kluntz steps up, goes through the rig-a-marole loading his antique, lifts her up like before and lets her fly. The beer bottle disappeared in a shatter of glass. No one cheered—they just looked at each other wondering.

"Looks like a tie," said Hal Parker.

"No god-damned way!" roared old Thomas Pelton. "Get a couple of whiskey shot glasses." Someone did so. Thomas walked out and put them on the end of a stick poked into the ground. The sticks were four-feet long, so the shot glasses could just barely be seen—shiny glass against the sky.

"I won't miss," said Charlie.

Thomas cranked a load in his lever action Model 64 Winchester and aimed, squinting down the barrel. His gun went off. We all looked.

"Clean miss," said Hal Parker.

"Damn, damn, damn," yelled Thomas.

Charlie Kluntz loaded his rifle with great care. He looked up at the target and sprinkled in a little more power and set the bullet just so. He walked to the line, brought his rifle up. His bobbing head did not hold very still and he put his rifle down again without firing.

"Ronnie," Charlie called.

Ronnie came forward carrying a one-quart whiskey demijon and handed it to his Pa (I guess it was his Pa).

"Kentucky sippin' whiskey," he said as he managed to get the bottle in his mouth and took a long swallow. "Ain't no good to gulp it as a rule." He stood around for a few minutes. This time his head stood still as he squeezed off. "Clean miss," said Hal.

"I shot too soon," grumbled Charlie. "Whiskey ain't worked yet."

Thomas Pelton was ready. He aimed carefully and I could see him let his air out slowly as he squeezed off. The stick just under the glass split and the glass went flying untouched.

"That is a miss," said Hal.

Thomas scowled, people mumbled.

Kluntz looked confident as he toed the mark. His head held still for him a full second as he aimed and fired. The little glass disappeared completely and the stick wobbled back and forth.

It was quiet for a minute.

"Hit," said Hal. "Charlie Kluntz is the winner fair and square."

It was still quiet when all of a sudden Thomas Pelton yelled out, "I'll be dipped in shit and rolled in tortilla crumbs." He laughed long and loud, shipped over to Charlie, slapped him on the back laughing all the more. "You damn chicken, you are the best shot I ever saw."

Then everybody laughed.

The tension melted. The people clapped him on the back, rubbed his shoulder and touched the rifle, Charlie Kluntz's smile could be seen all the way to Texas.

"Ronnie, bring the jug."

"Here gentlemen, Kentucky sour mash sippin' whiskey."

Thomas Pelton grabbed the jug and took a mouth full. His eyes watered a bit and he let out a long hiss. We always called it a whiskey hiss always loud and followed by a cough, if the whiskey was rough and ragged. This hiss was soft and pleasant as a lover's sigh.

The jug was passed around and around and around until it was empty.

"Got more," says Charlie. "In the wagon there." He pulled back a canvas to show a dozen or more quart-sized demijars.

"Dollar a piece." They all sold out in a few minutes. Lots of smiles and backslapping.

"Don't gulp it down men. This is sippin' whiskey. Please save the jugs for me. I will need them back. Just leave them over to the store."

Well, Charlie's pants were pulled way down by the coins in his pockets. The silly smile never went off his bobbing head. He was starting to go out the door when he stopped to watch two men arm-wrestling on a table. The smile left his face. He looked serious. When one arm finally went down, I saw him roll up his sleeve. His muscles stuck out hard as oak. His biceps were large, to say the least, and not to be outdone by his triceps or the muscles of his forearm. I noticed right off how long his forearm was—very long and a big advantage in arm wrestling. He started to head toward the table and I headed him off.

"No, Charlie," I said. "Been enough. Have a drink or two more and just relax and let it go."

He looked around the room like he understood something.

"Another day," he said.

Charlie did have a few more all right. Funny, the more he drank the less his head chicken-bobbed.

After a while Ronnie brought the buckboard up front like he knew what he was doing. William was hitched up, while Black Bill pranced around behind. Charlie rattled himself out, climbed into the back of the buckboard with Scrawny Ronnie driving. He laid his head down on he little saddle with he jug tucked under his arm. Before he conked out, he lifted his head, and moaned loudly, "Stud fee is two dollars. For Black Bill, that is. Mine is fifty cents."

Ronnie gave it a giddy-up and they were gone up the road a quarter of a mile and I could still hear him snoring.

Good-bye to Sweetwater.

About 1890.

Part IV

A Rodeo for Sweetwater

1

Late summer, evening time, when shadows were first growing long and the cottonwood leaves were painting themselves yellow and orange around their faded green faces, Tate rode into town. Tate was a cowboy. That could be told by the way he slouched in the saddle completely relaxed. A cowboy by the way the floppy, wide-rimmed hat was pulled down on his forehead to shade his eyes, and by the big red-and-blue bandana that made a triangle under his chin. A cowboy by the scuffed and worn pointed-toed boots, spurs and high-heels—boots that came up almost to his knees. A cowboy by the dirty checkered shirt, the hogleg pistol on his belt, and by his manner—by the way he looked and held himself, and probably by the way he smelled.

Tate rode a wiry, tough-looking mustang that was tired out with a drooping head and a slow plopo-plop through the dust. He was leading a mule carrying a pack. The mule looked spent but otherwise attractive as mules go. Tate was tired too. Spent would be a better word. A bushy gray beard covered his cheeks, chin and neck with his parched lips looking like his mouth had been poked there with a stick.

He looped his reins over the hitching rail after almost falling from his horse. He left the mule tied to his horse and stood.

His breathing was noisy and wheezy. He stood still for a while before climbing the three steps to the sheriff's office door. Without knocking, he shuffled in and sagged into a chair.

"Howdy-do, partner," I said.

"Howdy. Just a minute," he breathed back at me heavily just looking at his shoes.

When he more or less caught his breath, he looked up at me and said, "My name is Tate."

"I am Buck Fitz. You look like you came a piece."

"Oh, it warn't that far," he said. "I just ain't that sound no more. My damn legs and ankles swell up and my feet hurt inside my boots from the pressure. But," he paused, "God, I'm tuckered."

"You want a drink of whiskey, old-timer?" I asked, knowing he would.

"Why, thankee."

I handed him the jug and he took a couple of healthy gulps. He wiped his mouth with his dirty sleeve.

"Damn good skee," he said approvingly.

"Yeah, made local."

"You named Fitz?"

I nodded my head.

"Ever knowed a cowboy named Harley Fitz?"

"Sure did. That was my dad."

Tate sighed and took another small nip of my whiskey. He looked to the right, the left, and up and down like cowboys do before he ever looked at me again.

"He gone over?" he asked.

"Yes, he died five years ago.

"I bet he was shot by a jealous husband," he said with a chuckle.

"Nope, he just went to sleep one night and never woke up." Tate became restless, shifting in his seat.

"Best way to go," he said quietly. Then he just sat and looked off a while.

"Harley Fitz and I were kids together when we drove cattle up from Texas to Abilene. He were a top hand after while, but we were snot-nosed, green and raw when we started."

He paused wheezing again and said, "Yep, he were a good hand. An all around top hand." He paused again. "And a grand partner. I was hoping I could see him, but maybe you will do. What is your real name?"

"Marion," I said.

"Marion, did you know that was his mother's name?"

"Yep," I said.

"I'll call you Buck, then." He stirred again in his seat as I got another chair for him to put his feet up on. I started to pull off a boot for him. "No, don't do that, thanks. I don't think I could get them on again. Too much swelling."

"I'll tell you what cowboyin' was for the last fifty years if you want to hear. Your pop and I were the toughest and the best."

"Listen, old-timer, I do want to hear. Very much so, but you are about spent and probably hungry too. Why don't you bunk here? Pretty comfortable cot. No one been in jail for a long time. Bedding is clean."

"Obliged," he said, looking on the cot in the cell. "Just don't close the blamed door."

"I'll take your animals over to the livery stable and put 'em up for you. Maybe bring you some grub from Frances' Café."

I got up and headed for the door. He stopped me with a hand on my arm. "There's a couple of pack bags on the mule. Bring them in and throw them under my cot for safekeeping."

He was telling me, not asking me, but I felt very willing to obey his commands. Why? I don't know. It was just the way he was, and he rode with my father.

There were four bags on the mule. They were heavy and awkward. I could only carry two at a time, one in each hand, and barely that. I brought them in two at a time and dropped them by the cot. "These are heavy."

"Yep," he said back.

"What's in them?"

"Gold. Gold is heavy."

"My God!" I said, scratching my head. "Where did you come by it?"

"Honestly," was all he answered.

I just left him there then and led his animals to the livery where they were fed, watered, brushed and rinsed, then put away for the night. I went over to Frances' Café and got some steaks, beans, and cornbread.

"Frances, will you cut that steak up into small slices, you know, so they will be easy to chew." She didn't say a thing and did as I asked. I gave her some money and carried it over to the jailhouse. I had to wake Tate up, but he ate every bit, drank a little more whiskey in a glass of water. Then I helped him to the bunk.

"Yep, sure as hell, Harley Fitz's blood all right."

Then he was asleep.

I was very anxious to hear his stories in the mañana. I didn't sleep that night with a mind racing with wonder. Why the devil was he here now?

I came back early the next morning bringing Louise with me. Let me tell you about Louise. She is an Indian woman raised by a missionary doctor up in Nevada almost to the Oregon border, there. A Piute, I think. She went with that doctor everywhere. She studied his books and he taught her. When she was a younger woman, the doctor died, and she went back to live with the Piutes. She was naturally attracted to the medicine men and learned from them too. She was a natural healer with skill and insight. A homely woman, with a partial harelip even, she never married and was more or less feared by the other Indians. They feared her like a witch. When smallpox came to her village, she was forced to run away because they blamed her. Somehow or another she ended up in Sweetwater where she cared for the sick and even brought babies into the world. She accepted what people were willing to pay her. She was the only thing we had like a doctor and she did as well, if not better, than some real ones I have known. So I brought her to see Tate. Louise bent over him and put her ear to his chest feeling his pulse all the while. She examined his eyes and tongue and noted with concern his swollen legs.

"His heart is tired," she said. "He cannot eliminate the fluids in his blood."

"What can you do?" I asked.

"I can help him for a while."

"How long?" asked Tate himself.

"I do not know. Only God the Great Spirit knows. I will be back."

She left and I looked at Tate. He was sitting up because he got short of breath laying flat. He had a look of skepticism on his face.

"We don't exactly have a doctor here." I said.

"She'll do," he wheezed back at me.

I brought him some cornbread and coffee with three thick slices of bacon which he ate with appreciation.

"My horse and mule?" he asked simply.

"All cared for, don't worry."

"I wasn't worried. Just wondered."

When Louise came back she had a pot in her hand that she had boiled some seeds in and a bag of stuff that looked like leaves.

"What is that?" Tate asked.

"Boiled pumpkin seeds to make you make water and carry the fluid out of you. You must drink this, and some every day."[1]

She poured the yellow liquid in a large cup, and he drank

1 The origin of the modern diuretic hydrochorthiazide.

it all. Then she took a handful of leaves, moistened them and rolled them into a ball in her palms. She ended up making three of them this way.

"What is that?" I asked her.

"Foxglove leaves, other leaves, but mostly foxglove."[2]

She held them out and he took them one at a time, swallowed them whole and washed them down with a swig of whiskey.

"No more today. Swallow one ball every day."

Tate said he would do as she said; he was dying anyway. She laughed a little at him and turned to go.

"Ain't you goin' to beat a drum, rattle something and chant or sing or something over me?"

She smiled at him knowingly. "I do that at home," she said.

"Wait, Louise," Tate said digging in one of the bags under his cot. He came out with three gold nuggets the size of peas. She took them holding his hands for a moment.

"I feel good in you," she said seriously. "I hope my medicine will work for you, for a while anyway." When she got to the door, she turned and looked at me. "You have a big bucket for him. He is going to piss like a mule." And piss he did. I emptied that bucket ten times before supper. I noticed that he was breathing easier and his color was better. I also noticed the swelling in his legs was going down. He slept well that night, he said, and felt stronger. When Louise came back, she looked him over and said that his pulse was slow and steady and his lungs were not noisy. She said she was pleased. She made sure he swallowed the little green ball of leaves and drank another pint of the pumpkin seed juice.

She then stood there and put her hand out. I grinned.

2 Still used as digitalis leaf for heart failure.

Tate looked confused for a moment then dug out three more nuggets for her.

"Thank you," she said. "Take your medicine everyday."

When I came back the next morning Tate was up walking around and had just come back from emptying his piss bucket. He looked strong and comfortable. I noticed that he was barefoot. He caught me looking down at his feet.

"First time I had my boots off in awhile. Last time I couldn't even see my toes. My cousin Dirk had six toes on one of his feet and they were all grown together too. He looked like a duck and has about the brains of one, too, as I recall.

"I need a bath," he went on. "But first, take some gold, get some money from the bank and buy me a whole set of new duds." He wasn't askin' me. He was telling me. But I didn't care at all. That day was spent getting him over to the barbershop for a bath, a beard trim and getting him in his new duds. I had got him a big new bandanna that he tied proudly around his gizzard.

"What did you do with my old clothes," he inquired.

"I burned them just before they fell apart," I answered. He grunted at me is all.

"Supper is on me." he said. "Then I got things to talk to you about."

After supper we sat at the café with coffee that I spilled a little whiskey in.

"Where did you get the gold?"

"Came by it honestly."

"But where?"

"Don't matter none, I just got it. Lots of it. Apache gold."

He never told me more, and I quit asking after a while.

"Why did you come to Sweetwater?"

“I came here hoping to see Harley. I came here because I was dying of heart failure and there was something I wanted to do.”

“What?”

“I want to put on a real cowboy rodeo.”

“A rodeo?”

“A real cowboy rodeo,” grinned Tate.

“I wanted my old saddle bud, Harley, but you’ll do.” He looked at the ceiling a moment. “I mean you will do, Buck,” he said earnestly.

“Let me get this straight, Tate. You came to Sweetwater to put on a rodeo? That’s why?”

“Yep.”

“Why the hell?”

“Real cowboys like your pa and I are disappearing. Cowboys is disappearing too. I want to preserve something. No, that ain’t it. I want people to see the things we did and still do and want the hands to have fun showin’ off. Sounds a bit bizarre, I know. I want to tell you some stories.” He squinted out the window like he was looking at something far off. “I want to tell you true things that,” he looked at me with a pause, “maybe you’ll write down, but a good place to start is a rodeo.”

“Tate, you mean to use that gold, then, to put on the rodeo?”

“Prize money and the cost of building the facility, seats and shoots and all, as well as advertising all over the country.”

I just sat there with a lot of wondering going on in my head, but damned if I wasn’t putting plans together in my mind. Plans to build bleachers around a holding corral, a parade. Plans for sending the word out—all over—with posters and handbills.

REAL COWBOYS
SHOW YOUR SKILL
WIN PRIZE MONEY

Roping, Bronc Busting, Trick Riding

THE FIRST ANNUAL SWEETWATER RODEO

So I sat smiling, scratching my head and damn . . . planning.

2

Over the next couple of weeks Tate seemed to get stronger and looked a lot better. He took the ball of leaves every day and drank the pumpkin seed juice that made him piss. He told me that his death was delayed for a good reason. He was grateful but he wished the chest pain would quit coming when he walked too fast or too far or, sometimes, for just no reason.

We got the gold changed to cash money, over $24,000, then put it into the bank under the rodeo fund. We got the advertisements printed up and sent them all over I even to California, Texas, New Mexico, Colorado and Utah. The railroad gave us permission to use the big holding corral, and I began to plan the grandstand and bleachers. We picked a date. October 1st and 2nd, three months away. The town seemed to come alive with anticipation too. People are strange about liking to have some cause and something to look forward too.

So, anyway we had a good beginning all considered and, looking back at it all, it went well right from the git go and to the last hurrah.

Tate had moved into my place after awhile. He didn't like the jail much and my place was a little out of town where it was quiet. I had a lot of room because my wife had died and my offspring, a son and a daughter, had headed off to San Francisco. They wrote to me a lot, but they never came back.

After supper, Tate would start talking to me in a quiet but cheerful way, if his chest didn't hurt him too much. Sometimes he would get awfully pale and sweaty, but without complaining. I knew his old ticker was hurting. Sometimes he would take sips of laudanum out of this little bottle. He said that it helped the pain a lot, but sometimes he couldn't think straight so he used very little, really.

He was a natural storyteller. I never got tired of listening to him.

"Your father, Harley and I, came out of Texas from New York City. Bet you didn't know that. We was only twelve or thirteen and both were stuck in an orphanage 'cause both our mothers had died and our pas had gone off to the war to fight for the Union, and that was the end of them. Our relatives put us in the orphanage place because they were poor, dumb Irish and couldn't support no more young'uns. Harley found out he had an uncle on his mother's side that had a ranch down in Texas. Harley wrote to him. Pat Dunn. And old Pat wired back and said, 'Come down, boys, lots of room in Texas.' He would put us to work and teach us to be cowboys. Well, now we were two, excited, happy lads I'll tell ya. Quick as we could, we were on our way. I had two sisters, one older and one younger. Their names were Dora and May, respectively." (He would surprise me every now and then by his vocabulary and use of English.) "I felt pretty bad saying goodbye to them because I knew I would never, ever see them again, and I never did either.

"Harley and I went by clipper ship from New York to New Orleans. For three days we were both so sick I thought we would die, and they would just throw us overboard. On the fourth day we were well and hungry and put to work in the mess washing pots and dishes and stuff. It worked out good because it paid our passage and besides we got lots of grub. We made up for lost time, I'll tell ya. We even ate what people left on their plates sometimes and it was plenty. We got on a train in New Orleans, Louisiana, and went from there all the way to the end of the line and from there by freight wagon into Texas. Most of the time we had to walk behind pushing cows that belonged to the immigrants on their way west. They were good to us though. The womenfolks fussed over us some. They gave us hand-me-down clothes and shoes and fed us best they could.

"Let me tell you about what Texas was like then. After the war people were flocking in to settle. There were all kinds—Russians, Ukranians, and other kinds of bohunks, Irish folks, Germans, Italians and lots of Negroes who were freed slaves. We traveled with them sometimes. They treated us all right too. I learned at a young age that folks were folks. Some are good, but some are bad also and it ain't smart to put your trust in people you don't know. We got wise. We got tough and we learned to get what we needed. I remember one time Harley had a chicken stuffed in his shirt and was walking away kind of fast from the owner's wagon. The guy looked up at him from what he was doing and yelled after him, 'Young fella, you had better take that bird out of your shirt before it shits all over you!' Harley just kept walking all humiliated. It was too late though 'cause that bird had shit all over him under his shirt. He laughed loud and long, ending up by wheezing and wiping his eyes. We made it all the way to west Texas. We found out what pimps and whores, gamblers, con men, hustlers, crooks and fools were, and we didn't want to be any of them. We wanted to be cowboys more than ever.

"We got a ride in a buckboard out of Mason, Texas, to Dunn's Ranch. Manson ain't even there anymore. Washed out to the sea in a storm. There I met the finest man I ever knew. A big red-faced, half-bald, galoot with hands like a bear and a mouthy grin that could light up a dark room.

" 'Welcome, boys,' he says. 'Let's throw your stuff in the bunkhouse and get you to home. My God, you ain't got no gear! Where is your rope and saddles? Where is your boots and spurs? You ain't even got hats. What kind of cowboys are you.'

"I guess we looked plumb horrified. He let out with his famous laugh. You could hear it for a mile before he let us know he was kidding us. He stopped on the way and looked back at us trudging along behind him.

" 'You boys don't drink, cuss, take whiskey, smoke or chew or chase after wild women do you?'

" 'Oh, no sir,' says Harley. 'We're too busy runnin' from wild women with some preacher on our tail trying to save our wretched souls.'

"Dunn laughed all the more.

" 'We'll get along,' he says. And we sure as almighty hell did!

"He had us wash our dirty clothes and take a bath in a watering hole with a small stream coming and going in it. Then we had to sit around naked as white jaybirds while our clothes dried on the bushes. Some Mexican girls about our own age came by and we didn't see them till they were right on us. They laughed and pointed their fingers at us with their little fingers sticking out wiggling and indicating the size of our little peters. They chattered away in Spanish that we didn't understand. We were trying to find some cover behind sagebrush or anything until their mothers yelled at them and they left us alone. I was dead mortified and red as a rose, but Harley commenced to grinning and before long we were laughing just like those naughty little girls. Later on we got to be good friends with these girls. Ida, Marie, and Lou. We did a lot of things together like my first dance, my first kiss, and whatever. I always felt that I had no secrets from them. They sort of took us as we were, if you follow what I mean.

"Later that day Dunn took us in to the mercantile there in Mosely. (It ain't there anymore either. Blew plum away in a windstorm.) We got outfitted with new duds, belts, chaps, boots, spurs, bandannas, plaid shirts, and real longjohns. He bought us each a used saddle with a big horn and made sure that the leathers and cinches were in good shape. Now Harley, he was some shirt-tailed kin, but I was no one, you understand. I was very gratified and humbled down and, as I lugged my saddle out the door, I just started to bawl. Dunn, he understood. More than me, I think. He put his arm around my neck and gave it a squeeze that like to broke it, then he ruffled the hair on my head.

" 'You both goin' to be my boys. Hey, we forgot to get you boys a sombrero.'

"I never forgot it. How do you forget a kind, tough, rugged old man with hands like a bear, skin like rawhide, and a smile for the whole world to see."

Tate leaned back in his rocking chair and closed his eyes for a moment. I saw his lips mumbling something that I couldn't hear, but I got the impression it was some kind of a prayer.

"Tell me more, Tate, what did you do then? What happened to Dunn?"

Tate sighed loudly. "Hell, what we did. We busted our guts to learn to be cowboys so we could please him. We worked hard and never complained. We said a lot of thank-yous to a lot of good people along the way. Dunn assigned an older Mexican named Augustin to teach us. Dunn said he was the best all-around cowboy and horseman in all of Texas. That meant the whole world. In all my days I never met or saw another man like him, ever. But that's another story. As for Dunn, he lived until about eighty, I think. Died in his rocking chair on his front porch watching the sun go down. Never married. Never had any children of his own, that we knew of anyways. He always said he had a good ride out of life and that he had damn few regrets. Just before he died, maybe a month before, he told us that he was very proud of us. He told us that we were good honest men and fine cowboys and he hoped he was partly responsible. Then he said . . . ”

Tate choked up and dabbed at his eyes with the bandanna that was constantly around his neck.

“He said he loved us, me and Harley. Hell, I had to go to the barn and blubber but not before I told him I loved him too and kissed him on the forehead.”

He went on slowly and deliberately. “He left us the ranch which we had to sell out to pay debts we didn’t even know were there. There was some money left over and I gave it all to Harley except two hundred dollars. He needed a grubstake ’cause he was marrying Ida, and they were going to start a store in town where Ida taught school.”

“What did you do?”

“I got some new gear and saddled up for the long drive. I was trail boss in my twenties and making good money at it. Since I could read and write and knew math and arithmetic, I was paid four times what the average cowboy was paid just for keeping the records.”

“Weren’t you ever married, Tate?”

He paused a long time and looked at the window, the ceiling, the floor, the door and everywhere else but at me.

“Yes, I was married to Marie, Augustin’s daughter. She was the beautiful wild kind with Spanish eyes. She was a beautiful singer always asked to things, parties, churches and such to sing. She liked the attention and praise.” He paused again for along time.

“I had to go on the long drive to Abilene, Kansas, with nearly a thousand head. I really intended it to be my last drive. It was a lot of money for us and a good start. I told her I would be back in a few months, and I would send her the money, which I did. When I came home, I hadn’t even heard from her all the while. She was gone. So was the money, and I never tried to find out where she went. I heard, though, that she was in Los Angeles, California, doing well with some theater troupe. I just burned down our cabin and kept on going."

After a while he got up and started to get ready for bed. I just didn't know what to say so I didn't say nothin'.

"Tomorrow," he said, "I want to tell you about cowboyin'. I would like you to write it down if you would." It's the closest thing I ever heard that resembled a request from him.

I said I would.

"That's enough about me."

That wasn't nearly enough about him.

In the course of the next few days we talked. Rather, he talked and I listened. He made sure I was making notes. Evenings were spent like that while days were spent making preparations for the rodeo. Hell, I had nothing else to do as sheriff. It made me laugh that he wanted to make a dance platform. A big one, too, with a canvas top and a little stage for the music makers. It made me laugh, but it was a good idea.

One evening he kicked back after supper and started talking while I cleaned up (like I always did).

"Let me tell you about cowpunchers and horses," he said as he produced a small jug of good whiskey and a glass to sip it out of. He piled his big feet on the next chair and just motioned me to pull off his boots which I obediently did. He just grunted in the way of thanks.

"Are you ever going to tell me where you got the gold?" I asked already knowing the answer.

"Nope," he burped. "You know," he began, "there are lots of wild horses all over the west. Mustangs and sometimes barbis. All escaped from the first Spanish, and in 300 years they changed the way of life of the southwest and plains Indians. They say the southern Comanches were the first real horse injuns. They seemed always the best as far as I know.

They were not pets to them. They wore their feet out, starved them half to death in the winter and ate them when they had to. If they were on the run, they would ride one till it dropped, slit its throat, and drink the blood hot, cut off some meat, and grab another. For all of that they were trainers, I'll tell ya. They could tame the wildest broncs in just a few days. They taught me, the cowboys, how to do it. And ride. My God, they would tie loops in the mane so they could hang by their toes, ride on the side and shoot under the horse's neck. Bows and arrows too before carbines.

"Now when the cavalry came they did not like the rather smallish, wiry mustangs even though there were a few bigger barbi types. So, anyhow, they brung in some thoroughbred stallions that they cut loose with the wild stuff. Made a big difference after a while. The Mustangs could survive on the land and poor pasture, but they inherited some speed and size from the thoroughbreds too. When I think of a pure mustang I picture a short, tough-looking box of a horse with long mane and tail, dark-brown or blackish color with a box head, little ears and maybe a Roman nose. White ones were generally no good. Blue-eyed and poor eyesight. Got disease from the skin and even sunburn. That's right. We used to shoot the colts and mares on sight. Odd, come to think of it. Never saw no stallions or horse colts that were white. They were just the throwbacks mostly. Every now and again, a good one comes along I guess, but I never saw any. Indians didn't like them either 'cause it made them stand out as targets in battles."

He paused for a while, took another sip, looked up at the ceiling and began talking again with his eyes closed.

"Most boys had their own horses, at least two. It took four for the long drive north, so the company furnished the other two. When the cowboys was hired on, he put his horses out in the rumunda. Sort of meant he trusted the outfit. Lots of horses were rhonchi and half-trained. They always bucked a few times when the boys mounted up at first. They generally quit fighting in a few minutes and the good ones liked to go to work. They had to be taught to fly backwards when the ropes were flying out. They were taught to always face the rope by passing the lariat through the bridle. Sometimes a cow would run back, get the pony all tangled up, and all hell would pay. Horses, steers and cowboys all balled up together. Lots of cowhands got bad hurt and kilt from these doin's.

"We always drove in a bigger bunch than we could break 'cause we knowed that some would be just too damn wild and mean to ever be tamed good. The two-year-old male colts—males are called horse colts and females are called fillies—anyhow, we would cut them right away. It took three or four guys to throw the animal and tie, being all stretched out, then cut the balls off as fast as we could. We usually had to bum to the ends of the chords with a hot iron to stop the bleeding. We'd cover over the wound with tar and get 'em up right away. If they didn't get up and move around, they would lots of times die. Anyways, in about eight weeks they were a lot more docile as you would imagine. Trainable, mostly.

"We used bozels a lot to begin with. But when we could we changed to iron bits in their mouths because they were better controlled. The bits were a story in themselves. They have high parts, low parts, roller parts, long shanks, short shanks, extra long shanks, curb straps under the chin. The curb straps were usually rawhide but sometimes chain and wire were used too. The harsher the chin straps, the less harsher the bit had to be. Some cowboys were better at breaking and wrangling. It was kind of an art. They got good at it. They were good at bucken them out. They would put a sack over their eyes and they would just stand there blinded while the saddle was cinched up. Then the bronc buster would pull the sack off and away they'd go. These riders could stick like they were glued on. Every time the nag would buck they would quirt him hard in the ass until finally that old horse would learn if he didn't buck, he didn't get whipped. They would trot around a little confused-like then stand still shaking like a leaf in the wind. The wranglers would get off, handle that horse all over. Legs, feet, neck, nose and belly then climb on again for a second go-around which mostly was not much. They were rode every day for only a couple of weeks, then given over to some poor cowpoke to go from there. Half wild, really.

"I got to tell you about the best damn bronc bust I ever saw. He was a half-Indian, Comanche, I think, and half-negro. His father were an escaped slave. This guy was born on a horse I think and I swear he could talk to them. He always went a little slower when he could. You know, pet them, feed them, handle them all over before he got on. He would be leaning over them all the time with his weight on his elbows over their back until they got used to it. He would take them by a big rock to stand on himself, throw his leg over and sit there. Lots of times they didn't even want to buck. Saw it myself. Made the best horses too. If they wanted to buck, he'd take them out into the river where they couldn't get their heads down. I've heard of the northern Indians taking horses out in four-foot snow banks so that they can't get their heads down there either. It seems to take the fight right out of them.

"Old cowboy told me once his mother was about ready to deliver him out when they was jumped by some bad Indians. She jumped on a mare that was ready to foal. When they got far enough ahead, she jumped off, had the baby and the mare had its colt. The mama got back on the mare and he, the baby that is, got on the colt and they got plumb away."

He laughed at himself, got unfolded from the chair, took a swallow of whiskey and announced he was going outside to water the cactus. "I piss all the time," he said going out the door.

"Good for you," I said. "Watch out, you ain't got no boots on."

"Ain't goin' off the porch."

"I know that, just didn't want you to piss on your feet."

"My feet," he grunted from out the door.

The next night we were playing poker on the table for half pennies. He kept cheating openly and I would call him on it and he would just grin.

"You're dealing from the bottom."

"Hell, we already used the ones from the top."

At the end of the game he had all the pennies. He pushed them all back into the coffee can.

"Leave them there. We'll use them tomorrow. You can't play cards for shit, so we gotta start over.

"When the big trail drive started in the late 60s there were thousands of wild Texas longhorns running loose all over south Texas and into Arizona. They were abandoned by the Mexicans when they were run over the border during the Spanish war. Then the ranchers left them when they went off to the Civil War. They weren't like cattle, they were mean and wild animals with six-foot horns. Lots of times they would charge the horses and try to kill them. They hated mules for some damn reason. In south Arizona mule trains and wagon trains were attacked by wild bulls and destroyed! That's a documented fact. In the roundups to form trail herds to go up north we chose only young cows and calves. We had a hell of a go-around I'll tell ya. We branded all we could, roped them head and heel by teams, held 'em out, stretched 'em with our horses while another guy hit the hot iron to them and cut their nuts off. The full-sized bulls we shot dead. No good to us or anyone. We just skinned them out for the hides, took a little choice cuts of meat, backstraps, ribs and loins, then left the rest for the wolves and coyotes. They was a whole lot of Mexican wolves down there, I'll tell you. Damn things got almost tame being around folks. Coyotes, on the other hand, they lost a lot of their fear of man, but never hung around for long.

"The cowboys were teenaged kids mostly, skinny, poor fed from desperate poor families, mostly ignorant but then quite a few could read and write too. Some of the cowboys were released Negroes or escaped slaves. They were older guys and they made first-class trail hands. First-class cowboys in every way. They were grateful for their jobs and proud too. Seems that they were most often a lot happier. They were often smiling and complained very little. I was always glad to be with them on the trail. We were all partners together against the wind, rain and sun and dust and tiredness and soreness and thirst and hunger.

"Lookee here I have some pictures taken in either '89 or '70." He pulled an envelope out of his pack and put a bunch of pictures on the table. The first thing that struck me was how young they looked. The second thing was how skinny, scrawny and poorly fed they looked.

"On these trail drives to Abilene, we would go all summer without a cold drink of water. Lots of times we would have to suck the water through our bandanas or drink mud. Grub? Beans, dried beef and pork, beans, fry bread, bacon, beans, occasional fresh beef or deer with beans and maybe some biscuits. Watery coffee lots of times, and thick black tea. We always got berries and fruits when we could but I think some guys got a little scurvy anyhow. Oranges and dried apples, plums were a treat."

As Tate finished talking and dozed off again in his chair, I began to get a picture of how it was to be on the trail for months. Boys started out with their hands pushed down in their pockets acting brave but were really nervous and scared. They came back worn and tired with their thumbs stuck in their belts strutting around. Their sunburnt faces sporting stubble whiskers but with their chins in the air. They left boys but came back men. I started to understand what Tate was trying to tell me. In 1876, 322,000 longhorns were driven north and shipped to the cast from Kansas railheads. Between 1867 and 1887, only twenty years, five-and-one-half-million cattle were driven north. This drew settlers, storekeeps, and merchants to the region of the country that had long been thought of as, if not worthless, not worth the effort. Directly responsible for the development of the west were the true heroes. The cattle tenders of the west on their half-wild horses the American cowboy, a unique and mixed breed.

Let me tell you one of my own tales. In the early times two cowboy soldiers leftover from the war came into the territory together. Their names were Bert and Tom. Never did learn their last names. They started ranching right next to each other. They both worked hard and did pretty good for themselves. They brought their wives up from the east after a while. For some damn reason these women did not like each other very well and were barely polite to each other. Don't really know why, but I do know that at one time old Bert was sparkin' Tom's wife when they were young and Tom he was sparkin', well, he was sparkin' Bert's. I don't know what went on, but they both eventually married up with the opposite. Carol, that was old Tom's girl, first dumped Tom and then run off with Bert, and Bert's girl sacked him and went with Tom. Her name was Lucy. So anyhow, Lucy married Tom and Bert married up with Carol. Follow that? Kind of confusin', ain't it? Tom and Lucy had two kids and Carol had one. This was all about the same year or two. Lucy named her girl Lucy just like her and the son she named Russ. Old Bert he had a boy and he named him Carl. Tom and Bert were good friends for a while. Lucy and Carol just stood each other and stared at each other a lot. Funny situation. The two boys got along fine and were great friends, same dinky little school and all, while little Lucy just tagged along behind them with a dirty face and ragged, big-boy clothes on her.

Now there was a creek that ran across their two properties. Damn thing was dry most of the time. Bert needed the water for his stock, but Tom had another small source on his land. Bert saw fit to dam up the creek to store water in a muddy old pond and just left a little spillway going across to Tom's land. Tom took offense at it, which led to a lot of hard words and harder feelings. After a while, they weren't talking anymore, so it boiled down to the boys and the girl. They went to the same school but ignored each other completely.

Now Bert got sick and was about to die. He sent his boy Carl over to Tom's place to bring Tom back. Tom came with his two younguns tagging along on horseback. Bert was perched up in a chair on his porch, pale and wheezing. Tom tied his horse to the porch rail and clomped up the way to where Bert sat.

"Howdy, Tom."

"Howdy, Bert."

"Been a while, Tom," said Bert with a grin.

"That it has, Bert. Too long, I think."

Tom pulled up a chair and sat side by side not facing Bert. He lit a long, thin black cigar that let out blue smoke.

"You want one, Bert?"

"Hell no. Not good for my health," he replied with a grunt.

After a pause while neither spoke, Bert pulled himself up, coughed some and said, "We had a hell of a ride, didn't we."

"Yep, that we did."

After another long pause, Bert raised himself up a little further. "Why we mad at each other? I forgot."

"Course you wouldn't know, you old coot. You took my water."

"Oh yeah, that's right. You didn't need it. I did," says Bert.

"It were the principle of the thing. You didn't ask first."

"Would you have gone along?"

"Nope.

"That's why I didn't ask."

The two old boys sat for a while saying nothin', just staring out their bloodshot eyes at the land in front of them. Tom rustled around in the pocket of his coat and brought out a flask.

"Want a drink of whiskey, Bert?"

"Don't mind if I do. Obliged," he said, as he took a small swallow and handed it back.

Tom took it back and had himself a big swallow.

"Hey, Tom," said Bert, "you want I should break the damn dam up? I'll do it, if you want."

Tom got very restless, waved his free hand in the air and still without looking at him, addressed Bert in a matter of fact way.

"Nah, hell no, it don't matter none. Lots of things matter a lot more like you and I bein' friends for so long."

"Thanks, Tom. I need the water and I need the friend."

"Bert . . . " Tom started to say something, then stopped. In a while he waved his hand at the land in front of him. "We, you and me, we carved a chunk out of this, didn't we? Been a helluva ride."

"Yep," said Tom. "A helluva ride. I already said that. They say you're dying, Bert. Is that right?"

"Yep, that's so," said Bert.

"Where you want to be buried, then?"

"Hell, I don't care, Tom. Surprise me."

They sat quietly for a while then Tom took another big swallow and stood up and faced his friend. "I will tell your boy, Carl, that I will be here if there is anything they need.

Him and Carol. Anything I can do will be done."

"Thank you, Tom. You are a good man."

"Good-bye, cowboy," said Tom as he stepped away. He stopped, looking up at the sky, then turned around quickly and took Bert's hand, his other hand wrapped around Bert's neck and he gently pulled him to him with a long embrace. Without another word, he clomped off the porch, mounted his pony without looking back and started off at a slow walk. He waved his hand for Lucy and Russ to follow. They hadn't even got off their horses. They had just sat watching and listening. Down the trail, Tom stopped his horse and waited until his two children were up with him, one on each side. He wiped his eyes again and again with his bandana and spoke with a raspy voice like he was choking.

"A man's pride is a stupid thing when it goes wrong. A stupid thing. Shakespeare said, 'Friends of old and their friendships tried grappled unto your soul with hoops of steel.' "

He looked at each one of them. "Do one thing for me," he said. They nodded their agreement. "Never forget that."

Then he spurred his horse ahead. His boy, Russ, did not move but turned his horse around.

"Where are you going?" Lucy asked.

"Back. I have to find Carl."

"I am going with you," said Lucy. "He's my friend too."

After Bert died, his wife, Carol, moved back to Boston and took Carl with her to go to school in the east. He didn't want to go much, but then again he knew that it was a great opportunity. So they leased the ranch out and left one afternoon on a train from Phoenix.

Now it was four years later and he was back, Carl, I mean. His ways were different. He looked, well, soft. But he was big and strong, easy spoken, very polite and dammit, determined to take over that ranch of theirs and make it go.

He was pretty self assured. He was one handsome dude, too, and he knew that.

About a week before the rodeo, Carl looked me up in town. He was dressed like a cowboy with slouched hat, spurs, chinks for chaps, riding on an ugly roan pony with a Roman nose. He had an oversized forty-four strapped to his hip, and he was just right dirty.

"Hey, Sheriff Fitz," he says, shaking hands.

"Buck," I said. "Just Buck."

"Well, Buck, sir, I wondered if you could do me a favor."

"Forget the sir. What can I do?"

"I have my dad's .44 here. It is pretty new. I wondered if maybe you could teach me to shoot. I have a couple of boxes of .44s," he added.

"I ain't much with a pistol, Carl, I just carry this one for looks but I could get you started, I guess."

I was smiling from ear to ear at him.

"I shoot this," I said, picking up my Winchester .25-35. "Hell's bells, let's go to the dump."

We stepped out of my office onto the sidewalk and there was Lucy and Russ. Carl bumped right into Lucy and had to grab her to keep her from falling over.

"Pardon me. Oh, excuse me. I am very sorry," he said.

"You are Lucy aren't you? I am pleased to see you."

Lucy didn't say anything. She just stared at him like an angry cat.

"And Russ, I am so glad to see you again." He stuck out his hand first to Lucy who took it and shook it up and down once with a jerk. She wasn't used to shaking hands you see. Folks in these parts, well, we didn't shake hands with women much. When he turned to Russ, Russ was smiling like a sunny day, his hand already out, and shook hands like a man should, slapping Carl on the shoulder.

They all jabbered back and forth for awhile. Carl said he

was home for good and would like to see more of them. He was looking at Lucy when he said that and it didn't go unnoticed by anyone there. She brushed her honey-blonde hair from in front of her face and smiled pretty good herself, I'll tell ya.

"That would be nice," she said, then sort of looked at her shoes. It were cute. Silly word, but it were cute.

"Sheriff Fitz is taking me out to the dump to teach me to shoot this .44. Why don't you come along?" said Carl. With just a word more, they just said, "sure," together and off we went. The dump was behind town, north against the big hill. I left them talking and put a lot of bottles and cans up for targets with Lucy looking at Carl. When Lucy was looking away, Carl was looking at her and when Carl was looking away, Lucy was looking at him. They looked back and forth together very little eye-to-eye. It were cute. Russ went first. He shot his pistol six times and six bottles exploded.

I showed Carl how to hold the pistol with his elbow straight, supporting his wrist with the other hand. "Line the sights up exactly. Don't close one eye. Squeeze and don't pull the trigger. Keep both eyes open. Don't focus your eyes on the sights but on your target, then go ahead."

He shot six times all over the place with six misses.

"I'm going to find a rock to hide behind." Russ said good-naturedly.

Everyone laughed but no one laughed harder than Carl himself.

"Show him what he is doing wrong, Russ. Hell I can't shoot a pistol either and hit anything."

Russ took the pistol from Carl, reloaded it and handed it back looking kind of serious, "When you sight-up don't look at the gun or the sights like Buck says. Focus your eyes on the target and practice lining up the barrel in your mind's eye. Takes a little practice," he added.

Carl did as instructed. It took him three loads, but finally he was hitting four or five of the six shots.

He was grinning and proud as hell of himself and it showed. Lucy had been watching with a rather blank expression. “Buck,” she said, “Let me have your rifle a minute.”

I handed it over knowing what was coming. The bottles were all broken with just the pieces left. Well, she brought that rifle up and cut loose as she could. The glass flew. Every time! When the gun was empty, she handed it back to me without even a smile.

“Thanks,” she said as she turned and walked away toward town.

I could see a giggle in her shoulder, even from behind and she kind of skipped a little.

Russ looked like nothing special had happened.

Carl? Well Carl looked like he was proud he knew her, but there was more in his eyes. There was more.

3

The dirt street in front of my place lay sprawled out and covered with dust waiting for the morning sun to begin the daily baking. Somewhere an early morning rooster crowed his daily challenge to the day. A few other small birds flew over and in a small flock not saying anything to each other. Too early in the morning, I guess. Not awake yet.

The old cowboy sat on the porch sipping a cup of coffee from a clay cup. He glanced up to me when I came on the porch. "You sleep all day?" he asked matter-of-factly.

"No, I don't." I replied immediately.

"Made some decent coffee. Get yourself some and sit a spell." Again, it was a damn order not a request.

I did as I was told and sat down in the other rocker. The coffee tasted like it was made with mud, and I thought it might melt the enamel off my teeth. He saw the look on my face.

"Trail coffee," he commented.

"You should have left the trail out of it," I said.

"Huh?" he grunted back, not understanding

After a while sitting in silence he began to stir and like before he was ready to talk. Before he began, he motioned me with his eyes like usual, so I got up and got my big tablet and a pencil. He looked satisfied then and after a couple more sips and a sigh he began again.

"Cowboys never owned much, you know. Almost all were single guys in their late teens and twenties. Almost none ever thought they would be at this job for their life and, as a matter of fact, damn few were. Most boys owned a horse or two, a saddle, a rope, spurs, an oilskin slicker usually a poncho and a pair of boots. On the spurs the big rowels were called California spurs in Texas and Texas spurs in California. Damned if I know why. In Arizona I guess they could be called either way. Anyway, every cowboy had his spurs. He rarely took them off and knew how to use them to good advantage on a reluctant horse. Their poor damned bedroll was just rolled blankets wrapped up tight in a canvas bag. Lots of boys were packed off and buried in that bag." He paused and his eyes were wrinkled, "If they were dead, of course," he continued.

"Now most cowboys didn't even own no pistols. Some had .44s but they were heavy and they didn't always carry them. Bullets weren't all that cheap or available and no one could hit anything with the damn things anyway. Lucky ones had Winchesters or sharps rifles and even old military breech loaders. They kept them in the bunkhouse or wagon 'cause stuck in the saddle, they could get tangled up in the bush or with a rope. They came out usually for hunting purposes. Sometimes for just traveling though. Sometimes.

"Never saw a gunfight in forty years. In camp anyway. People did strange things in towns, so that don't count none."

He chuckled to himself some which led to a rough cough that was punctuated by spitting a goober into the dust.

"I learned to read at a young age and I read every damn thing I could. I had bags of books to fill my head and prided myself always on learning more. I learned a lot but I sure didn't learn everything or enough."

He sat back and stuck his thumb in his belt, gazing off at a single white cloud, not passing by, just sitting alone in the sky. I knew his story was coming.

"In 1880 or a little later I was running an outfit in East Texas. We were gathering up all the critters we could, getting ready for the long drive in the spring. There were six of us, counting the cook. The cook usually had a helper but this galoot got drunk too many times and I ran him off. Never did figure where he got his tequila. We found it hidden all over after he left. Poor hombre had a disease. Alcoholism, but I couldn't do nothin' about that, so the cowboys were made to pitch in and help cook. They didn't like it none but they had to anyway. One evening just before supper after all the cows were either laying down or staying together grazing and all was quiet, we spotted a rider coming from far off in the south. We stood watching as finally he trotted up and stopped by the chuck wagon, tied his horse by the reins, and walked over. Greenhorn. Number one, guys don't tie their horse to the chuck wagon, ain't done. Dangerous and could get in the way of a lot of things. Also, you don't tie a horse that pulls back like this one did by the reins. Well, I ignored all that cause he looked like a fuzzy-cheeked, dirty boy.

" 'Howdy,' I offered up.

" 'Howdy do. This is the D Bar T outfit, see. I'm looking for Tate. My pa says that he knowed him and he would give me a spot.'

" 'I am Tate,' I says. 'Who's your pa?'

" 'Calvin Hanks. He is daid now but he told me sometime before that you'd probably give me a job 'cause he knew you. My name is Jedediah. Jed Hanks.'

" 'Oh, yeah,' I says. 'I remember Calvin Hanks, (but try as I might, I couldn't remember him). 'I'm sorry for your loss. He was a good hand.'

" 'Can you take me on?' he asked a little desperate.

" 'Come, sit down. I'll get you a plate and a cup. Eat.' I looked around at the boys and rattled off their names knowing or thinking anyhow that he wouldn't remember any of them.

" 'This here's Hank, Red, Lou, Boyce, Terry, Mike.' They

all waved a little and commenced to eating their bacon, beans, dried plums, biscuits and coffee.

" 'Come on, kid,' said Hank, the cook, while he heaped his plate up.

"That kid was hungry, I'll tell ya. He gobbled it all down, and the cook half filled his plate again.

" 'Thank you, thank you, sir,' he kept saying. Now nobody ever called the cook 'sir' before, and he liked it. You know, as long," a sigh and a long pause later, "as long as that boy was with us, he called Hank 'Sir.' Me, he just called Mr. Tate or 'boss.' I saw the cook untie his horse from the chuck wagon and tie him with a small, short rope high on a mesquite branch. Later we taught him principles, 'tie them high, tie them high, tie them short and not by the reins.'

" 'I want to be a cowhand,' the boy began. 'I have my own horse, saddle, rope, and all.'

" 'You got any experience at it?' I asked. He never stopped looking at me in the eyes, I mean, so while I knew he was gonna be that well . . . I dunno, I knew he was gonna be all right. Know what I mean?

I really didn't, but I nodded my head so he would continue his story.

"The kid and I reached an agreement that we would take him on as a cook's helper, part-time wrangler, and we would teach him cowboyin'. That is as we could and how's time permitted. He was real eager to start so he jumped up, ran over to the cook.

" 'What do you want me do first, sir?'

" 'Jed, boy, gather up all the plates and cups, wipe them and the empty pot out with sand real good, then take them over to the creek there for a wash. Here's a rag and some soft soap. Be sure and rinse all that soap off.'

" 'Yes, sir.' He stopped part-way to the boys.

“ ‘Who’s the wrangler I’m supposed to help?’ he asked.

“ ‘That’s me,’ says Lou standing up.

“ ‘You’re Lou,’ the boy said. ‘I’ll check in with you when I’m done. I’ll be a lot of help. I know a lot about horses and I can ride like hell.’ We all smiled. But, he was right. He did and he could. Surprisingly. Someone had taught him well and he was talented.

“Now his horse it was a big raw-boned thing with lots of hair around the ankles, hanging over the hoofs. Near as I could tell, it was a cross between a light plow horse and one of them thoroughbreds. Turned out to be one of the best ropin’ horses. The boy, Jed, he spent a lot of time training him, but that horse was willing too. Faster than you would think and strong. And Jed practiced every free moment he had.

“We were several weeks, months really, before trail time. We had herding, roping, branding, castrating, and sometimes shooting and skinning to do before we would be ready. Jed was out there all he could be after his camp chores were done and the ramada cared for. He had a good attitude and the boys nicknamed him Little Jed. They liked him.

“Now you know how men are with younger boys. They tend to tease a lot. Too much. My boys were no different and sometimes they seemed a little mean. I would not put up with that and without Little Jed knowing it, I put an end to, well—excess. Criticism and fun-poking that wasn’t all that kind, anyhow. It was good-natured tricks and laughing remarks that went on that were appreciated by Jed too. I remember one time Little Jed left a half a cup of coffee laying by his plate while he went to fetch another biscuit or something from the fire. Lou reached around and filled it with whiskey. Little Jed sat down to finish eating and everyone was watching. Little Jed took a little bite of biscuit and a big spoon of bacon and beans chewed for a while, and in a minute drew a big gulp of coffee to wash it down. He swallowed, swallowed again, his eyes watered and got big. Presently, he wipes his mouth with his sleeve and said, 'Best goddamned coffee I ever had.' I want to tell you, we all about split laughing. No one laughed harder than Little Jed.

"I think Red was hardest on him. Not really hard, but not very friendly and ignored him. Red was the best roper and all-around cowboy there except me, of course, but try as he might, Little Jed couldn't get through by being polite and even doing extra little things for him. One day we quit early in the afternoon. We were all gathered around talking about the trail coming up and such. 'Got a few cows and calves out, about ten or twelve,' I said. 'Broke away from the herd and need to get herded back. They are down in the gully by the wash. Red, it's your turn. Take Little Jed and get them in.' Now Little Jed was eager for real cowboyin' and action. He jumped up, grabbed his rope and headed for his horse that we now called Clodhopper. Red got up, too, but slower. He grumbled that he was tired but he didn't need no fuzzy-cheeked little peckerwood, pot washer to help him. 'Send a man or no one,' he said.

"Jed stopped in his tracks, dropped his gear and ran at Red with his arms swinging. His fist thumped on Red's shoulders and chest and belly. That surprised Red. He was so startled that he just stood there taking it. Then finally he pulled his hands over his face and brought his elbows together over his belly.

" 'I'm sorry, I'm sorry. Don't hit me no more.'

"To further dramatize, he started coughing and gagging. The show was funny but no one laughed. No one was fooled except Little Jed who was all filled with himself like a prairie chicken rooster. He strutted over and got a ladle full of water, brought it back and gave it to Red to drink. Damn, damn, damn, no one laughed, but I didn't know how anyone could help it. Anyways, no one laughed out loud. Somehow I saw what the books call 'tears of mirth' in their eyes, and I thought I was getting soakin' wet. Red, he gathers himself up and says kind of loud, 'Come on Little . . . Come on, Jed, let's get them wild ones in.'

"You know, I was proud of Little Jed, all right, but I was a helluva lot prouder of a cowboy named Red.

"Soon after Jed joined our outfit he found that there was an old gut-string guitar in the front of the wagon. No one knew who it belonged to but I thought it was our former cook's helper guy. Anyways, I told Jed he could have it. In his usual modest way he told us he could play it perfect. He could play it damn well but not perfect by any means. He could sing too and seemed to know a lot of songs. The ones I had never heard I found out later he had wrote. He would sing along low then slip into that high voice, a falsetto, then end with a yodel. He got a lot of them cowboys singing along too. I guess you could fairly say he was one well-liked, dirty-faced, fuzzy-cheeked, scrawny little leftover maverick.

"Which reminds me of something. You know why cowboys sing to the cows? It's because cows can be so damned jumpy. If they don't know where you are at night, and you come up and startle them, they're liable to stampede. Singing lets them know its just old you coming along.

"I always thought cowboys yodeled cause they were imitating coyotes."

Again he chuckled at his own joke. "Don't leave that out," he said. I nodded my head and made a big thing of writing it in. "To go on, Red and Little Jed got to be first class pardners. Red was in his twenties and I knew he had had a hard life growing up as an unwanted stepchild of a mean and vicious, drunken old German immigrant. Red told me once that when he was just fifteen and a half, himself a big person already, he waited until his step old man got a little drunk, then beat him up good. Kicked his ribs and then lit out. He told me he had no use for his mother either because she never tried to stop the abuse. Anyway, one way or another, he turned out to be a fine man, a top hand, and later on a successful rancher and politician. But, that is another story, one worth telling. He took Jed under his wing, so to speak. He taught him all he knew about cowboyin' and made Jed read to him and the boys out of all my books.

"I want to tell you about cows. Particularly wild, longhorns. They are nervous, jumpy, not very content. They startle and scare easily then they can stampede and run for miles trampling everything and everyone in their way. The only way that they can be stopped is by turning the leaders back on themselves in a circle. That is one of the devil's own hell-pissin' dangerous endeavors that cowboys had to go through. Don't always work. The worst thing is thunder and lightning. Times like that the whole crew rides out and around singing. Sometimes it works, sometimes it don't.

"One dark afternoon when black clouds hung close to the ground and the wind and rain came together, we knew we were in for it. All hands went out. We tried but when the thunder and lightning hit, them beeves lit out. They lit out like they was running from hell. There was a blind canyon ahead of them, but they would have to be turned. We all prayed a lot out loud. Some of it didn't sound much like Sunday school prayers. We got some boys in front of them, shouting, waving stuff, and the guys with guns shooting. Damn if those cows didn't turn pretty as you please into that blind canyon where we had them tucked up safe. We were a mite proud of ourselves and after guarding the entrance all night, we took turns going back for hot coffee and breakfast at the morning's first light. Red and I had just pulled up and were reaching for the coffeepot.

" 'Where's Little Jed?' I asked Red. Red looked around at a couple of boys who were leaving back to their post.

" 'Anyone seen Jed?' he asked. No one had. It was eerie quiet for a minute. We both dropped our coffee and headed out. First we went to the cowboys on post. No one had seen Little Jed after the start of the run. Lou said he saw him in the lead when the turn started.

"Red and I and Lou headed over there.

"We found Clodhopper standing head down with a leg broken above the ankle and the bone sticking out. Over his head and down a little gully Little Jed lay face down with his head at an odd angle. Lou and I couldn't move. I thought my heart would stop dead still because it was broken. Red swung off his horse, went down on his knees and lifted him up, turning him over so he could look into his face. He held him like you would hold a little kid.

" 'Goddamn, son of a bitch. Goddamn, Oh Goddamn, oh Goddamn. Oh why? Why?' Red blubbered, shook and wept. My heart broke the rest of the way and I couldn't stop bawling. Lou hid his head in his hat and shook all over.

" 'Why? Why, why, why,' Red kept saying. 'Oh, Goddamn. Why? Why?' Red came up holding Jed loosely. 'Why, why, why, Tate,' he demanded

" 'I don't know why. He didn't suffer, Red. He died right away.'

" 'Why? Dammit it to hell. Why?'

" 'Don't swear no more, Red. I don't know.'

" 'You read all those damn books,' he said again. 'What do they tell you?'

"Between my own choking I managed to say, 'They tell me that sometimes there just ain't no why.' "

We sat on the porch then and I understood what the old cowboy wanted me to do. Their times were hard, their rewards were few, their appreciation little, their importance was immeasurable, their courage grand but their camaraderie was grander still.

"The story is not really over yet. There is more, but it is better for another day," he added.

"I don't want to wait another day, old cowboy Tate. Tell me the rest," I asked.

"Well, there is really no rest, so to speak. Get me another cup of this good coffee, will you? Hey, and spill a little whiskey in it to settle the mud.

Again, obediently, I did as ordered. I poured the cups half full and the rest with whiskey and brought them out. He took his with a grunt and slurped up some.

"Kind of stingy, weren't you?" he muttered.

"You must have got mine. Sorry, I'll get you some more."

"No, no this will do." He sat there for a while watching a day full of nothing, yet finally he said, "Buried him in his bedroll on the greasewood flat. Somebody, Red, I think, put a flat slab of wood for a marker and burned into the wood.

——JEDIDIAH HANKS, COWBOY——

"We took all his gear off poor old Clodhopper, then put him out of his misery with a 30-30. That sort of mended things for a while."

"Here's the odd part. About no more than two weeks later I came into camp to find a girl with a dirty sunburned face and sodbusters sitting down with cook for a cup of coffee. She looked a little familiar. She had very bright, wide-open, shiny eyes, blue as cornflowers. Dirty blondish hair hung down all around her head to her shoulders. Damned if she weren't a cute little thing anyway, even with a dimple. As I got off my horse I glanced at the one she had ridden in on. It looked like Clodhopper's twin. I knew who she was before she even spoke.

" 'Tate, my name is Lottie Hanks. I came looking for my brother Jedediah who I understand is working for you.'

"I didn't say a word.

" 'I need a job too,' she said searchingly.

"I went over to her and she surprised me by sticking out her hand to shake. She had a good-natured smile on her face. I took her hand, but I didn't let go.

" 'Sit down here, Lottie,' I said quietly. She knew something wasn't right so sat herself awkwardly down on the big rock. I looked all over. Up and down, right and left, in front and in back before I could even look at her. 'You was Jed's little sister then?'

" 'Mr. Tate, what do you mean "was?' "

"The cook disappeared and left me just telling her as easy as I could. We all liked him. He was a good cowboy, a good-natured boy and we all missed him. I ended by telling her he did not suffer at all and, God knows, we were so sorry.

"Tears made little river streaks down her dirty face. She just cried softly to herself and my heart just ached for her.

" 'Can we go see where he is at?' she asked quietly.

" 'Sure, little sister. But for now, why don't you get cleaned up, get some food in you. Try to get a night's sleep. It is late evening and it gets dark quick.'

" 'Thank you, Mr. Tate. I appreciate you looking after Jed and being kind to him and me.'

" 'Just call me Tate or boss,' I said. 'Jed just called me boss.'

" 'I'll call you boss, too, then. I have to take care of my horse.'

" 'We will take care of your horse, little sister.' Somehow she smiled.

"She was back at supper time. All the guys knew the story by then. They were all kind of polite. Red, he was very careful to tell her that little Jed was his partner and how he was so sorry and missed him. Lottie looked into his eyes and saw the sadness there. All the while she, herself, looked like she would like to comfort Red in some way.

" 'Thank you, Red Ballow, you are a good man.'

"She poked around at her supper not looking up much. Red found a bunch of meadow hay and another old quilt and made her a nice bed under the wagon.

" 'I'll take you there to his grave in the morning,' Red said kindly as he showed her to his nest.

"What happened then, Tate?" I asked. "Where did the girl get to?"

"You ain't one damn bit romantic if you can't guess."

"Oh," I said and sat down again.

Tate looked eager to finish the story. "Yep, Lottie stayed on as cook's helper, even wrangler helper and did a good job too. Red he was smitten polecat, I'll tell ya. There was a lot of grinning and good natured little whistling going on at Red, but he could have cared less. Before it was time to go on the trail drive they came to me to say that they were going to get hitched, Lottie got a job in the only store in town to wait for him to come back from Abilene with a hat full of cash. You see Red, he knew arithmetic and could write good and he could keep track of the cowboys. We were all very happy especially me because I knew she would wait. She would be there waiting, he would come back, and they would do well."

With this Tate stood up, brushed himself off a little, finished his coffee whiskey and walked into the house without looking back at me. I knew the story was ended and so I left walking slowly into town.

4

Big Louie had a ranch outside of town that he used to run wild mustangs. He brought a large black stallion in with him that he said was to be used in the rodeo. The black stallion was large, much larger than the run-of-the-mill mustangs that wandered the hills. His front shoulders were strong and his chest was wide with deep heart and well-formed withers, straight back and heavy quarters that bulged with muscle. He was surprisingly light on his feet and danced about sometimes with only one foot left on the ground at a time. A throwback, I decided, to the original barbi horses brought in by the first Spaniards, built and bred to carry men and their armor. He was wild. I mean wild. Somehow Louie had captured him when he drove in a band of mustang mares. He had to install an extra height of rails to hold him in his corral. No one could get anywhere near him. He would lash out with his front feet and extend his neck with his teeth bared and would bite whoever he could. None of the cowboys would attempt to get too near him, let alone break or ride him.

Louie was torn between shooting him and letting him loose. He knew if he let him go, he would run off some of his good mares and probably raise hell with the fences. He couldn't bring himself to shoot him. *He's just too damn beautiful*, he thought. He didn't want to release him either so he kept him, and when the rodeo news was brought to him, Louie saw his way clear. He let out the word that he had the meanest, toughest, orneriest and wildest horse in the world. He would give him to the rodeo and put up twenty dollars to anyone who could stay on him for a half a minute. As he looked over the big animal, he smiled to himself and even chuckled. *My twenty dollars is safe*, he thought.

When time came for the bronc riding, everyone knew of the horse and had come by to see him. There were low whistles and quiet remarks of appreciation for his size and strength and his wild-eyed meanness.

Russ looked him over, quietly alarmed that he could not even make eye contact. When he tried to touch him in the small shoot, the black devil almost bit him and managed to rip off a piece of his sleeve.

"My God, where did you come from?" That was all he said as he walked away. Carl came too, stared and whistled but didn't try to touch him. He first looked on him with wonder, respect and a little fear too.

"I'm going to try to ride this guy?" he asked himself. Others looked, everyone looked. Rudolpho came up with his sombrero in his hand and said something in Spanish that made the beast snort, blow and toss his head. He left without looking back with wonder in his face. I think that the most significant man to come up and look was Tate. He wheezed up to the pen on his puffy legs and rested his chin on the rail. He didn't speak for a long time. When he did, he made sucking and chirping sounds with his lips and talked slow and quiet. The horse turned his head and looked at him and I noticed that his eyes were soft, not at all wild and bulging. I saw Tate put his hand on his neck and hummed to him. He patted him, and that damn nag not only let him but looked like he appreciated the attention. I don't know. I noticed Tate being around for quite awhile. When I came back again to check on things, Tate was still there, and Señor Negro that we called the horse was eating hay. As it happened only Carl, Russ and that Mexican guy, Rudolpho, who was a friend of the roper from California, agreed to ride.

In the center of the arena was a big snubbing post. With two ropes around his neck and walking hobbles on, the big black was finally brought close enough to be snubbed with his head high. A sack was rapidly put over his head and the animal stood still quivering, blinded by the sack. A saddle was prepared to be safe as could be for bronc riding. The stirrups were large, wide and almost round. If a cowboy caught his foot, he was dead. The saddle was light with a sturdy wide girth, strong belly girth and a low-rolled cantal, just deep enough to bury your buns but low enough to swing off when the time came. If it did come.

Carl was first. He gently lifted the saddle onto the back, no blanket of course, buckled the belly girth just touching the skin. Then the girth was kicked over from the front behind his front shoulders. Carl grabbed it, secured the latigo with four wraps and tightened the girth as tight as he could. If the saddle got loose, oh boy! Anyhow when he was ready, he put his left foot to the stirrup, grabbed the mane with his left hand and swung aboard. When he found the right stirrup with his right foot, he pulled the lead rope up and wrapped it twice around his hand.

He leaned back, let out a sigh and said loudly, "Let him unwind!"

The snubbing rope was released and the blind ripped off simultaneously. The large horse stood only for a moment, then reared up so far he almost fell over backwards. He pushed off with his hind feet, leaving the ground with a high, forceful buck then lit with a bone jarring crash, all four feet hitting at the same time. Carl was already in trouble being jerked forward and off balance. Black horse rose hard, all four feet off the ground, kicked out in a buck then twisted in the air, coming down in almost the opposite direction. The next buck loosened Carl and he flew through the air like a human cannonball landing flat on his face in the dust. His wind was knocked out, as he lay struggling to inhale. The horse casually bucked away.

Two cowboys rushed over to Carl and lifted him up under the arms. He accepted the help with as much poise as he could muster.

"What the hell happened?" he said.

"You fell off, cowboy."

"Hell's bells, I never fell off a horse in my life. I was thrown thirty feet, fair and square."

As he hobbled away the big black was roped again by two cowboys. With the rope both tied around his neck, they got him back to the snubbing post and put the black bag over his head and he stood pretty still.

Russ walked up then, confident as only a fool cowboy can be. He checked the girth and stirrup length, found them to his satisfaction, and got on. When he was ready he yelled, "Let him go!"

Well, he let go all right, first he stood in one place, spun on his hind feet, first in one direction then in the other so fast it made me dizzy to watch them, exploded with a twisting, spined up, four-legged buck that came up in the east and went down in the west and with a sideways rolling buck and a loud snort, he rid himself of old Russ. It was kind of funny to see. Russ flipped all the way over and lit in the sitting position with his arms waving in the air like a bird.

He got up on his own, said nothing and hobbled off by himself rubbing his lower back and ass as he went.

You know what? That cabillo was hardly sweating and I swear he had a smile on his crazy white-eyed face!

He got caught up again, not even trying to fight the ropes that checked him and came right back to the snubbing post where the routine was repeated.

Rudolpho walked around him looking him over. He adjusted the stirrups to fit a much shorter man, tested the latigo, tied the strings from his sombrero under his chin and smoothly mounted up. When he was ready, he didn't say anything. He just nodded his head and leaned back in the saddle as far as he could.

That horse went wild. He was not tired. He sun-fished, lurched, twisted, spun, crawled the air, heaved himself up, jarred himself down. He squealed and snorted and farted. But Rudolpho stayed with him. Hell, no one was timing anything by now. The big black was finally getting tired. You could tell. No horse could keep that up like that for too long. His bucks and his heaves and twisted motion became weaker and weaker until he was just jumping around. Then he stopped, stopped dead, still shaking with his chest heaving and sweat dripping down his face.

Rudolpho flew out of the saddle landing gracefully on his feet and let go of the lead, grabbed the sombrero off his head and bowed deeply in all four directions with his left arm swinging out each time like some dancer. Everyone laughed and shouted compliments. Rudolpho never changed the look on his face at all. He put his sombrero back on his head and sat right down on the ground and wiped his face with his bandana. A bunch of cowboys, the Texans, Carl and Russ rushed over to him and tried to lift him on their shoulders.

"Dios! I would rather walk than ride now," he said in broken English.

Later, when things quieted down, Rudolpho stalked up to Louie.

"How long I ride?" he asked.

Lou checked both his hands. "More than a whole damn minute. I lost track. You got twenty bucks coming, man," Louie laughed loudly and handed Rudolpho a twenty-dollar gold piece and a slap on the back.

"Señor Louie, do you want that cabillo?"

Louie looked him up and down, "Hell no, I don't want him."

"Will you sell him to me for this twenty dollars?"

Louie stopped where he was going and looked at the earnest look on the Mexican's face, "No." Louie paused a long time, "I won't sell him at any price to you. He is yours. You can have him." Louie walked away without looking back or acknowledging the young man's thanks.

Damndest thing I ever saw. Rudolpho led that black Roman-nosed critter over to the entry gate into the arena. He opened the gate, and quickly slipped the rope halter off both of the horse's ears. Before it was completely off the stallion broke and ran full speed away. Damndest thing I ever saw, that horse stopped a hundred yards out, turned hisself around, reared up, pawed the air and let out a stallion squeal that would scare the devil himself. Then he was gone.

Tate was leaning on the fence near by. I never saw a bigger smile on any man. I heard Louie mumbling to himself, "My God, he's gonna run off a whole bunch more of my mares."

5

Tate and I wandered down to the rodeo grounds a couple of days before the rodeo. We were kickin' around the cattle pens building a starter chute for the calves; while watching two cowboys working on it, a Black fellow walked up with four of his friends tagging along behind him kicking the dust.

"My name is Nat Love. I came over from New Mexico for your rodeo," he said quietly.

"Glad to have you," responded Tate with a grin. "What is your best job?"

"Ever heard of bulldoggin'?" the cowboy asked.

"That's where you wrestle a steer down off your horse, ain't it?"

"Sure is. We ride beside the running steer, come off the side, grab his horns and nose and throw him over. The other guy hazes to keep him running straight. Good show," the Black man added.

"Well," said Tate, "we weren't plannin' on it but it sounds real good."

"We can show you one time if you want," he said eagerly.

"Why not?" says Tate. The chute was finished so the five cowboys selected out the proper-sized calf with one-foot-sized horns and roped him out and drug him bawling into the chute.

"Good chance to try this out," Nat said.

It was strong and well made and the chute held the cow well. Nat got on his horse and rode over to the left side while his partner on a small black mustang got himself lined up on the right. I got behind the calf with a sharp stick.

"When you're ready, sing out," I said.

Nat and the other cowboy adjusted themselves in the saddle. I noticed Nat took his left foot out of the stirrup.

"Let 'em go!" he shouted.

I opened the chute and stabbed the steer in the ass. He jumped out and took off running full speed. The hazer on the right kept him going straight while Nat crowded up, leaned well out of his saddle, grabbed on to the horns, set his heels into the dirt and twisted. The steer tumbled over on his side and Nat let go when he was down.

'Nice job," says Tate happily. "It is a good show. Who you going to compete with and how you going to score," he asked.

"You scores by the time it takes and all these galoots with me are bulldoggers."

"All right then," Tate says after looking them over. "I'll give thirty dollars to the winner and twenty dollars to the second place."

"Nope," said Nat. "Fifty dollars for the winner and twenty-five for the second place time."

After a pause he added, "It's a hell of a show and dangerous."

After another pause, "Done," said Tate.

Everyone shook hands all-around and the grinning cowpokes wandered off toward town.

"You could have got it for forty dollars and fifteen dollars," I told him.

"I know it!" he replied with a snort.

Russ, Carl and Lucy were there looking around when a California Mexican pranced up on a beautiful palomino. He said his name was Tim Sanchez Ortega and he did lots of rope tricks and calf roping. He had a huge smile on his round face. He was colorfully dressed, wearing a pair of blue pants with a red sash and a white shirt.

I spoke to him in my very best Spanish and asked him to show us a few tricks. He snaked out his riatta that was forty-feet long at least and fashioned a loop that he spun completely around his horse, up over his head, down the sides and then in front of his horse. Damned if that horse didn't jump right through the loop and Sanchez brings it up spinning over the horse's rump.

"I'll be," said Tate. "You do that for the show? I'll pay you . . . thirty bucks."

"I told him cuarenta, forty bucks," I said.

"I do a big show on the ground also?" he said like a question.

"All right, keep the show going off-and-on between the rides and stuff all day."

"Fifty dollars," he said in English.

"Fine," said Tate. He looked at me wisely. "I speak Spanish too," he said. "Could have had it all for forty."

Lucy had watched and expressed her pleasure with his skill, clapping her hands. I saw two West Texas cowboys saunter up and look her over smiling at her in a too-friendly fashion. One pulled himself away, and swooped over to where Sanchez was retrieving his outstretched riatta.

"Let me see that magic riatta," he said grabbing it up and out of the dust.

"This here is new rawhide. Why I bet you could still make soup with it."

He pulled a big knife out of his waist sheath and acted like he was going to cut it. Fast as a whip, Tim Sanchez jerked the riatta from his hand, sending the knife flying.

"Hey!" yelled the cowboy and bent over stumbling around looking for it. When he stood up, Tim had recovered his rawhide rope, made a loop and sailed it out over his head. Sanchez snugged up around the cowboy's knees and dallied around his horn. His horse flew back and jerked the protesting man off his feet. Every time he tried to get up, Sanchez yanked him back again sending him sprawling. It was a pretty good show. The roped cowboy soon was laughing like a clown and protesting way too loud and too much.

"You got me roped. Are you going to brand me? For God's sake, don't make me a steer."

I watched his partner laughingly reach over and put his arm around Lucy's waist. She struggled to get free but he held on. Carl was right there in his face. "Let her go!" he shouted.

The cowboy looked kind of surprised and glared at him.

"All right, polecat," he said, as Lucy slipped away. The cowboy threw a roundhouse right that would have taken Carl's head off if he hadn't ducked under it. It became apparent that Carl knew how to box. I mean box like he had learned at school back East, not just punching. I stepped forward with my rifle posed to speak.

"Let him be," said Tate with a knowing grin.

I put my rifle down and watched.

Carl circled around punching straight ones right in the cowboy's face with only his left hand until the guy's nose was bloody. The roundhouse swings of the cowboy were futile as Carl just dodged and ducked under them. That West Texas guy never landed a blow.

"All right, all right, you win," the Texan pulled his bandana out, began dabbing and wiping his now pretty bloody nose. Carl put his hands down and looked over at Lucy who was watching wide-eyed and silent. He never saw it coming. That cowboy let loose with a right across Carl's head that sounded like a mule kicking a pumpkin. Carl went right over on his back and lay there dazzled and dazed trying to shake the ringing out of his ears, trying to focus his eyes and trying to get to his feet.

The Texan stood over him, pinching his nose with his bloody bandana.

"Hell, man, never let your guard down like that. I could have hit you real hard and hurt you."

With that statement the cowboy went behind Carl, put his hands under Carl's shoulders and sat him up gently. Carl just sat there shaking his head. You could almost hear the bells ringing. Lucy ran over and put her hands on Carl's cheeks and began kissing him on the face, forehead and cheeks. Carl shook his head and finally grinned.

"My hero." Lucy said with a laugh.

"Miss, I apologize for my bad manners and disrespect. I don't do well in towns. Whiskey, you know. My pardner, Chet, he don't either. I had better get him undone." With this the wiry Texan went over to his partner and helped him out of the rope.

"You are ready for brandin'. Where's your knife. I am making you into a steer right now."

The cowboy, Chet, jumped to his feet, kicking the rope away and walked quickly over to where Sanchez sat on his horse coiling his riatta.

"Hey, Pedro, I wouldn't have cut your riatta, I was only funnin' you. That is the best I have ever seen. Beautiful work. I'll give you thirty dollars for it. After I win it in the rodeo."

"No," says the Mexican.

"How much you want for it?"

"Fifty dollars."

"All right. It is worth it. After the rodeo when I got some money."

Tate turned to me, "I wish we could put the show we just seen in the rodeo entertainment," he said as he walked away.

When the day came around everything was ready. The arena and seats were all finished and waiting. The dance floor was ready too and looked real nice. Many people had come to town and were camped all along the river. The Indians camped a ways further down the river with their ponies herded together grazing on the only grass around. In the rodeo the Indians won all the horse races (which was really a good thing).

We started with a parade right through town. The contestants were led by buckboards, hay wagons, carts and bicycles all decorated up and painted. Everyone who could play an instrument was going at it. Children were laughing and running along with their barking dogs out front. On a big black horse with a white blaze across his face and a fancy saddle sat Tate. It was funny how serious he looked. All this was furnished by Russ and Lucy's dad. He was as wrapped up as anyone in the festive occasion and he had a smile on his face that you could see for miles.

The rodeo went on for two days, with a parade each day before the show, and a dance in the evening. Everyone was in good humor. The music was pretty good. By the last day there were a lot of cowboys there with cracked ribs, bruised faces, lame legs, slings and sore butts. I watched Carl and Lucy dancing. It was pretty easy to see what was going on there.

"Bully," I thought.

Tate was doing pretty well, but I knew his chest hurt him and it was hard for him to be cheerful.

"I am going for a walk down to the river," he told me. "Thanks for everything, pardner." He turned and left before I could say anything, but I managed to pat him on the back as he left.

The old man wandered slowly to the edge of the river where he clutched his chest slowly and slid down by a cottonwood tree. He watched the stars for a while before he closed his eyes.

"I got no complaints," he mumbled before he slept.

When peace came in its special way to the old cowboy, a horse whinnied somewhere in the distance, a coyote howled out his song to the night.

Out of the rusting frame a younger body stepped out with a bright smile and a quick step. He waved to the stars and to the moon, saluted his former body, then walked off not looking back until he disappeared in the mist from the river.